MYSTERY
of the BELLS

MYSTERY
of the BELLS

by
VARDINE MOORE

Illustrated by
ALCY C. KENDRICK

Philadelphia
THE WESTMINSTER PRESS

Library of Congress Catalog Card No. 55-7794

PRINTED IN THE UNITED STATES OF AMERICA

To my husband
Robert Bruce Moore

CHAPTER

1

Fᴵʀᴇꜰʟɪᴇѕ ᴡᴇʀᴇ ᴊᴜѕᴛ
beginning to flicker in the twilight when Tony Parker
strode out the back door followed by his sister, Cherry.
Silently she followed him down the path and through
the white picket gate that divided their back yard from
the well-kept garden at the back of the big white house
where their friend Bentley Adams lived.

For most of her ten years, from the time she could
toddle after him, Cherry had been following devotedly
in her older brother's footsteps. Tony never objected.
Even when he and Bentley had become close pals,
Cherry was always welcome, for she could run like a
boy and climb like a boy and never pulled any girlish
tantrums.

Tony, now twelve years old, had all the dignity of his
real name, which was John Frederick Parker. But the
nickname had stuck to him since the day long ago that
Captain Gabe Fellows remarked: " Here comes Tony
Rooster strutting like a prize Banty. If I still had my

boat, I'd like to take that lad down the river for a mascot." From that time on, everyone in the neighborhood called him Tony.

When the gate closed behind them, Cherry pushed back a stray lock of brown hair that curled softly about her face. " What do you suppose Bentley wants to tell us that's so important? "

" Your guess is as good as mine." Tony shrugged his shoulders. " All I know is what he told me on the phone. He said to come over as soon as possible for a meeting of the Be Dramatic Club, and he sounded kind of excited."

Matching her steps to his, Cherry wagged her head seriously. " It's a good thing we finished our dishwashing job in a hurry. Mother didn't have to say a word about dawdling this time."

" Let that be a lesson to you," Tony chuckled. " Just shows what you can do when you keep your mind on your work. It took less time than it usually does to decide whose turn it was to wash and whose to dry. Come on, let's hurry."

They broke into a run across the smooth grass and were pacing along the driveway beside the house when the soft pad of prancing feet caught up with them.

Tony whirled around and stopped on the back of his heel. He pointed a stern finger at the small dog looking up at them with pleading brown eyes. " So! You squeezed under the gate again. You'd better get back home, Skippy. Go right back the way you came."

The brown-and-white markings on Skippy's back stood out distinctly in the fading light as his plumy tail waved like a feather fan.

8

"Oh, please let him come with us," Cherry begged in a wheedling voice. "I know Bentley isn't very fond of dogs, but I'll hold him and I'm sure he'll be good — won't you, Skippy boy?"

As if he understood her words, the dog's slowly moving tail fanned furiously.

"All right, Skippy," Tony grinned. "You win. Only be sure to mind your manners and don't go chasing shadows all over the yard and making Bentley nervous."

Walking on beneath the lighted windows of the living room, they rounded the corner of the house just as Bentley sauntered out the front door. Bentley Adams, tall and thin as a bean pole, seemed guaranteed not to wrinkle or show soil. His fingernails were never grimy and his fair skin always had a well-scrubbed look.

"You finally got here, I see," he said, coming down the steps and walking toward the white iron bench swing that hung from a limb of the spreading oak tree. "Want to sit in the swing with me, Cherry? Room for two."

"Thanks. I'd better sit on the grass with Skippy and keep him out of mischief," Cherry answered demurely as she seated herself on the ground with the dog curled at her side.

"Wonder what's keeping Lynn?" he murmured impatiently, as he backed into the swing and motioned Tony to join him. "I have important news for the club, but since she's the president, we can't very well start the meeting until she gets here."

From the grim set of his face, it was evident that the news was serious — perhaps even unpleasant. But before Tony or Cherry could ask any questions, Lynn

Wilson came swinging leisurely across the lawn toward them. She was a small, wiry girl with crisply curling black hair and a bounce in her walk.

Watching her approach, Cherry felt a warm glow of happiness. She had been delighted when Lynn moved from New York City with her mother and dad into the new apartment building down the street, just half a block from the Adams house. Until that summer, there were no other girls in the neighborhood, so Tony and Bentley were her only companions outside of school friends. Boys were fun, of course, and they'd always had good times together, but every girl needs a special chum, and she and Lynn had hit it off right away.

There was first of all the nearness of their ages. As Lynn said, " I may be small but I'm going on eleven." Cherry admired Lynn's lively ways and her boundless enthusiasm for introducing new projects. It was her idea to organize a dramatic club, and she was elected president. The club met in Bentley's large basement game room and used it for their auditorium.

" Greetings and salutations, fellow players," she called out in a singing voice. " Why the long faces? "

" Bentley has news for the club," Tony explained as Lynn brushed at her red pedal pushers and flopped on the grass beside Cherry and Skipper.

" Sorry I'm late," she smiled, stroking the dog's brown-and-white head affectionately, " but Dad has just come home from one of his long trips and we had a lot to talk about. He brought me the prettiest white sweater with two French poodles on the front, one embroidered in black and one in red."

" Who ever heard of a red poodle! " Bentley snorted. " Sounds repulsive."

" Everything sounds repulsive to you, Mr. Adams," Lynn retorted loftily. " Let's have your important news."

Bentley cleared his throat self-consciously and hesitated as three pairs of eyes searched his face. " You see — " he began, and swallowed hard. " It's like this. We can't use our basement for rehearsals or shows any more. My folks are planning to make a fancy rumpus room or recreation room there, and they — well — they don't want a lot of kids running in and out."

" Well," Lynn said, snapping off a short blade of grass, " then I guess that means the final curtain for our dramatic club, and just when we were getting such a good start."

The air was heavy with antagonism between Bentley and Lynn. There were times when she had a way of putting him on the defensive, and it was distressing to Tony and Cherry each time their two best friends flared out at each other. They noticed Bentley's cheeks flushing hotly at the sharpness in her words.

" Don't worry." Tony broke the uncomfortable silence. " We'll find another place."

It wouldn't be easy, however. Their own basement was little more than an old-fashioned cellar, and they all knew that Lynn had no place to offer. The basement of the apartment house was shared by several families. Of course she was disappointed. They all were.

The Adamses' game room was a perfect place for their meetings and dramatic productions. There had been only one public performance, billed simply as

"The Magic Show." Bentley, as the master magician with a bagful of magic tricks, was the star attraction. Cherry and Lynn had charmed the audience with baton-twirling and tap dancing. Then Tony performed a lively tumbling act that drew enthusiastic cheers from young and old alike, and the show ended with a short dramatic skit in which they all took part.

The entertainment played one afternoon last week to a capacity house. Indeed, the Standing Room Only sign went out before the opening number. Now, it looked as though there wouldn't be any more performances of the Be Dramatic Club for lack of an auditorium.

"We could use our cellar — " Tony began hopefully. "But it's too little. Just about big enough for the furnace and for Eloise and her kittens. Besides, everything gets mildewed down there."

"Except Eloise and the kittens," Cherry giggled.

Tony smiled at his sister's attempt to ease the tenseness with her ever-ready humor. Then he grew thoughtful as his eyes lifted with a faraway gaze. "If only Captain Gabe were still living, I know he'd let us use his carriage house. He always let us play there until he took that plane trip and never came back."

The others followed Tony's gaze across the street to the big old red-brick house on the hill where Captain Gabe Fellows had lived for over fifty years. Now it was empty, waiting lonely and majestic for someone to live there again.

"Just what is a carriage house?" Lynn asked curiously.

"It's a vine-covered brick building at the back of

13

Captain Gabe's home that he called his carriage house, although he said it hadn't covered a carriage nor housed a horse for years."

" I guess it's an old-fashioned name for garage," Bentley suggested. " Nowadays, such a building would be for automobiles instead of horses and carriages."

As they looked toward the beautiful home of the old river boat captain, through the maple trees that lined the long, curving driveway, the white columns reaching two stories high shone eerily in the darkening shadows.

A subdued silence fell like a mist, and Skippy crept under Cherry's arm. With his head in her lap, he began to flick a small red tongue at her hand.

Bentley shuddered. "How can you stand to have that canine lick you? "

" He's no canine," Tony stated firmly. " He's just a plain mutt. Captain Gabe said so when he left him with us."

" ' Canine ' means dog," Bentley laughed in a superior manner. " Whether he's a mutt or a thoroughbred, he's still a canine."

" That's true," Tony said, relaxing a little toward his friend. After all, Bentley was probably feeling pretty scratchy inside. " Skipper's just a plain mutt but Captain Gabe loved him. He asked Cherry and me to take good care of him when he left on his trip."

" And now you have to keep him," Bentley persisted.

" Of course we're going to keep him," Cherry put in quickly. " We love him too. When Captain Gabe's daughters, Mrs. Winslow and Mrs. Ackerman, came here from the East to see about things, they told us

14

we could keep Skippy forever. He's our dog now."

" He's a nice dog, too," Lynn said, scratching Skippy's ear. " Just wish I could have a dog, but you know how it is in an apartment. The only pet we have is a parakeet. But Kim is fun and smart as he can be." She broke off suddenly. " And now about that carriage house — sounds like a wonderful place for the club."

She jumped lightly to her feet. " What do you say we take a look at it now before it gets too dark? "

Skippy hopped from Cherry's lap and began leaping around gaily, ready for action.

" We'll have to ask permission first," Cherry replied. " Tony, you take Skippy home so he won't run off and have us chasing him after dark, and ask Mother and Dad if we may go across the street and show Lynn the carriage house."

" Sure. This way, Skipper."

As Tony hurried off with the dog scampering at his heels, Lynn called after him, " Please phone my mother and ask her too."

Tony nodded in agreement as he rounded the corner.

" I wonder if anybody's ever going to live up there again," Lynn mused, her eyes straying back to the house on the hill.

" My dad says nobody can live there until the estate is settled," Cherry explained, choosing her words carefully. " Captain Gabe's will left everything to Mrs. Winslow and Mrs. Ackerman. But it was a very old, faded will and there's a later one someplace, but nobody knows where it is."

" How do they know there's another will? " Bentley asked.

" Because Mrs. Jackson, who was his housekeeper, said so. She and her son witnessed it before Captain Gabe left. She said he wouldn't have forgotten George, although she didn't read the will."

Lynn's eyes sparkled with lively interest. " Who is George? "

" Captain Gabe's son. He adopted him after his daughters were grown up and married. He's overseas now in the Navy."

" He was wonderful to all of us kids," Bentley said with a sudden bright smile. " I remember how hard he worked teaching me to ride my first two-wheel bike. And when he played the piano, he'd invite me to come in and listen sometimes. I was sorry when he went to New York to study music at the conservatory there."

Tony came running up in time to hear the last remark. " Who're you talking about? George? We haven't seen him for a long time."

" I remember he never wore a hat," Cherry smiled dreamily. " He always reminded me of a Greek god with his curly golden hair."

Tony gave his sister an amused sidelong glance. " Cherry! How you talk! A Greek god is a statue — one of those things carved out of stone or something." He turned to the others. " George wasn't like that. He used to bring us baskets of eggs at Easter, all wrapped up in colored cellophane."

" I wish he'd come back here to live! " Lynn exclaimed, clapping her hands together in a burst of enthusiasm. " If he is as wonderful as you say, he'd probably be glad for us to use the carriage house."

" Not only that." Tony grinned. " I expect he'd even

16

become a member of the club. And you're going to get to see the carriage house right now — at least from the outside. Mom and Dad said we could go over and show it to you if we'd hurry back. We will, because they're going to take a walk and meet us here, and your mother invited the whole crowd up for hot-fudge sundaes as soon as we get back."

"Good! Let's go." Lynn linked her arm through Cherry's. "Is everybody ready?"

Bentley hesitated. "It's beginning to get dark," he objected.

"There's nothing to be afraid of," Cherry assured him. "There's nothing up there but sleepy birds and katydids and a few harmless squirrels."

"You're not afraid of the dark, are you?" Lynn teased.

"No, I'm not." Bentley turned abruptly. "Wait a minute. I'll run in and tell Mother where I'll be."

After he had left them, Lynn asked Tony, "Do you think he's really afraid?"

"I think he's just upset," Tony replied loyally. "He must feel at odds with the world because he had to tell us we couldn't use his game room any more."

"I think we ought to show him that we don't hold it against him by being extra nice to him," Cherry added.

They heard the sound of the screen door closing, and Mr. and Mrs. Adams walked down the steps with Bentley running ahead of them.

Mr. Adams, a comfortably plump, fun-loving man, waved jovially to the group as Mrs. Adams, tall and thin like Bentley, with smooth dark hair, tilted her head in an apprehensive, birdlike manner and called out: " You children hurry back. We'll sit here in the swing and wait for you."

Following the wide, curving driveway, each one felt a curious excitement, but Bentley trailed reluctantly, casting side glances into the dense shrubbery as the sound of their feet crunched in the gravel. When they drew near the big house, they were greeted by the chant of cicadas and katydids clacking like a dozen busy typewriters.

The air was heavy with the acid odor of fading mimosa blossoms mingled with the sweet scent of tuberoses in the garden between the main house and the carriage house, which loomed darkly ahead.

" I'm going back," Bentley muttered. " We can't see anything."

" Oh, yes, I think we can," Tony said, swinging ahead, " when we get out from the shadow of the trees. Come on."

From behind them, Bentley let out a sudden terrified yell. " Hey! There's a light up there in the window."

Turning around hastily, they saw him pointing to the second floor of the old brick house, which was now shrouded in total darkness.

" There was! " Bentley shouted. " A flashlight! "

He fled at breakneck speed down the driveway, with Tony, Cherry, and Lynn close behind him.

Mr. AND MRS. PARKER
enjoyed a slow evening stroll around the block after
Tony had put Skippy safely in his outdoor pen and
rushed back to Bentley's through the hedge gate.

As they walked along the tree-lined street, a soft evening breeze blowing up from the river ruffled Alice
Parker's short curly hair.

"I think we're the happiest family in the whole
United States of America," she said, giving her husband's arm an affectionate squeeze. " Maybe in the
whole world."

" No ' maybe ' about it, my dear." Mr. Parker smiled
down at his wife. " ' As a man thinketh in his heart, so
is he.' "

" We have a comfortable home, good health, and we
have each other," she began enumerating, like a child
naming particular joys. " And Tony and Cherry both
have special chums of their own. They're having a wonderful summer together. That little Lynn Wilson is

full of pep — I might say a wee bit too peppery at times," she smiled, " but I think she and Cherry are good for each other."

" You mean Lynn may give Cherry a little more spunkiness — she's always played second fiddle to the boys — and Cherry may calm Lynn down a bit? "

" Something like that," his wife answered in an off-hand manner.

" I think there's going to be a moon tonight," Mr. Parker said suddenly. He pointed toward the river. " Look — can you see it shining over there through the trees? "

They stood quietly for a moment to look at the moon coming up, round and golden, and then walked on.

There was a feeling of contentment in the quiet neighborhood when they stopped for a visit with Mr. and Mrs. Adams. Greetings had just been exchanged when Bentley came running pell-mell into the yard, followed by Tony, Cherry, and Lynn. They were breathless and panting, more with excitement than from exertion.

" Well, you certainly got back in a hurry." Mr. Adams laughed dryly. " Did you show Lynn the carriage house? "

" No," Tony admitted somewhat sheepishly. " Bentley thought he saw a light in Captain Gabe's house, and we ran."

" I *did* see a light! " Bentley's voice was shrill and insistent. " A little flitting light, like a flashlight."

Mrs. Adams searched her son's face with her usual worried expression. " Are you sure, Bentley? Are you really sure about it? "

" Sure, I'm sure." Bentley sounded impatient. " It was just for a second, but I know I saw it. Right in the upstairs front window."

Mr. Adams brushed his hand lightly through the air as if to dismiss the whole idea. " Sounds highly improbable. You know you have a vivid imagination." He turned to the others, a slight smile on his full lips. " Did any of the rest of you see this strange, mysterious light? "

" No," Cherry said in a voice just above a whisper, as Lynn shook her head slowly.

" But we tore out of there anyway." Tony brushed at his back hair with an embarrassed grin. " It seemed like a good idea at the time."

Cherry was beginning to feel sorry for Bentley, who stood silently with downcast eyes, digging the toe of his shoe into the soft turf. And then she caught the calm, steady expression in her dad's eyes. He had a way of making every situation smooth.

His voice was deep and gentle. " Bentley is probably right. I have a hunch that he saw the reflection from the lights of a passing automobile."

Mrs. Parker was quick to add reassurance. " Of course! Why didn't we think of that sooner? Wouldn't the headlights of a car turning the corner at the top of the hill shine in that direction? Bentley could have seen the reflection caught by a mirror in the room."

" There's not much chance of anybody getting inside the house. All the doors and windows are locked securely." Mr. Parker's words had an encouraging ring. " But just to be sure, we'll go up and take a look around. Captain Gabe left a key with us, and the court

21

authorized us to keep it in case of an emergency. This isn't an emergency, but I think a checkup might be in order."

" How about going with you, Dad? " Tony asked eagerly.

" Sure thing; we'll all go. Wait till I run over home and get the key. Be back in a jiffy."

" Don't forget a flashlight," Mrs. Parker called after him as he rounded the house for the short cut through the hedge. Then she explained to the others: " All the utilities are turned off in the house on the hill. There's no electricity, gas, or water. A good scout always carries a flashlight in the dark. Right, boys? "

" I'll get my flashlight and go along too, if I may," Mr. Adams suggested, his round face animated with the prospect of adventure. " We'll make a game of it."

Mrs. Parker agreed heartily and the plump figure scuttled into the house just as Lynn's father came down the street looking for his daughter. After hearing the story of the strange light, he offered to join the investigation.

When everyone was ready, Mrs. Parker and Mrs. Adams decided not to go. " Too many cooks spoil the stew," Mrs. Parker laughed. " We'll walk on up the street and let Mrs. Wilson know where you are and what's causing the delay."

" Tell her to hold the hot-fudge sundaes till we get back," Lynn said, taking Cherry's hand.

" Coming, Bentley? " Tony asked as he noticed his friend hanging back.

" No, thanks. I don't think I want to go."

Tony felt disappointed and looked toward his dad.

Maybe he could persuade Bentley to come along.

Mr. Parker's smile was full of understanding. "That's right, Bentley. Somebody should stay and walk up the street with the ladies. I'm glad you thought of it."

Tony was glad that his father hadn't suggested that *he* stay behind. Although he knew the checkup was only a routine procedure, he wouldn't want to miss it for the world, and his pulse quickened with the excitement of adventure as the cheerful group went swinging along the driveway to the big house.

The full moon had risen above the treetops and shed a brightness that made their flashlights unnecessary. There was laughter and gay exchange of banter as they walked completely around the yard, carefully observing the windows and trying the doors. But all laughter ceased and a quiet hush fell when Mr. Parker fitted the key into the heavy lock on the front door.

As it swung back silently, Tony's heart beat faster at sight of the wide hall with the familiar winding stairway. A long view was revealed from the front to the back door, where moonlight shone through the large pane of glass.

A complete survey was begun of the downstairs, first the long living room on the left, then the paneled dining room on the right with a big, old-fashioned kitchen at the back. While the men were flashing their lights into every corner, Lynn silently admired the handsome, spacious rooms where Cherry and Tony had spent so many happy hours with their friend Captain Gabe.

Without discovering anything unusual, they circled

23

back to the front hall and Tony peered curiously into the living room. " It sure looks ghostly in there," he muttered. " Wonder why all those white sheets are covering the furniture? "

"They were put on when Mrs. Winslow and Mrs. Ackerman were here," Cherry explained, "to keep out the dust."

"Looks awful spooky," Tony went on. "Smells haunted too, all musty and stale."

Mr. Parker flashed his light through the archway. "I expect it's about time for us to come in and air out these rooms," he observed. Then, turning to Mr. Adams and Mr. Wilson, he explained, "It's our job to open the windows and give the place a good airing every few weeks."

"Our particular job is to fill the birdbaths in the garden," Cherry told Lynn as Mr. Parker turned and led the group up the winding stairway. "Captain Gabe loved birds and told Tony and me to keep water out for the cardinals and robins and catbirds and mockers. He called them his boys."

When they came to the top of the steps, Mr. Parker looked around thoughtfully. "Now, let's see. We'll look in the Captain's study first. That's where Bentley saw the light, wasn't it?"

"That's what he said," Tony answered gravely. "In the upstairs front window. The study window would be the one nearest the place he was standing."

The three men went in ahead and, after making a complete search, were convinced that the small room was undisturbed. Lynn, gazing from the doorway with wide-eyed interest, could see many glass-framed pictures on the walls and the tall, antique desk that stood near the window. It was richly carved and designed with numerous cubbyholes and drawers. Her attention was caught and held fascinated by the beautiful model

25

of a river boat displayed prominently on the topmost part of the desk.

Before she could make a move to enter the room for a closer inspection, the men filed out and Mr. Parker was closing the door. " No signs of an intruder," he announced with firm conviction. " Bentley must have seen a reflection from headlights shining on the glass of one of the pictures on the wall."

" I'm sorry Bentley stirred up so much trouble," Mr. Adams apologized, shaking his head with a perplexed frown. " I don't know where that boy of mine gets his hairbrained ideas. I never saw anybody with such a wild imagination."

" There's no harm done," Mr. Parker assured him. " I would say the boy is very observant and someday he may uncover something of real importance." Walking across the hall, he continued good-naturedly, " We'll take a look through the rest of the house and then I'll be satisfied that it was just his imagination this time."

It wasn't long until the group was ready to return with a confident report that all was well in the house on the hill.

" Bentley's probably dying of curiosity," Tony said to the girls on their way back.

" And I'm dying for one of those hot-fudge sundaes Mimi promised," Lynn replied, turning in at the tall brick building with an eager bounce in her step.

Following close behind her as she led the way upstairs to their second-floor apartment, Cherry whispered to her friend, " It sure is nice of your mother to invite all of us to come in for refreshments."

"Oh, Mimi loves to have a crowd of people and fix up something good to eat. She was born in Texas and grew up with a houseful of brothers and sisters, always having company."

Just then Mrs. Wilson appeared in the open doorway of the brightly lighted hall. The sapphire blue of her dress exactly matched the deep blue of her eyes. "Did you all scare away the spooks?" she drawled, a broad smile on her friendly, sun-tanned face.

Lynn puckered her mouth with pretended disappointment. "There weren't any spooks or anything. Wouldn't you know it? But listen to this, Mimi!" She grabbed her mother around the waist with an excited hug. "I wish you'd been with us! You'd love that house — great big rooms full of antiques and — "

"Wait a minute, honey," Mrs. Wilson's soft drawl interrupted. "Invite your guests in and then tell us all about it."

The living room of the Wilsons' apartment was friendly and cheerful with the soft glow of lamplight on polished antique wood, burnished copper, and gay-flowered chintz. Everyone was made to feel at home and welcome immediately.

When all the guests were seated, Mrs. Wilson tied a ruffled rose-colored apron around her waist. "Now, please, please don't tell everything until I come back from the kitchen. I don't want to miss a word."

"There's nothing much to tell," Mr. Parker smiled. "We made a circuit of the house inside and out, and everything was just as we left it several weeks ago."

"Then I'd like to hear more about the place," she insisted. "It looks so interesting, I've been curious to learn more about it ever since we moved here."

Lynn touched her mother's arm lightly. " Could we eat first? I'll help you to get things ready and I can tell you something about it while we heat the fudge."

Cherry offered to help too, and the chatter of their voices mingled with the clatter of dishes from the kitchenette.

In a few minutes they were back again, Mrs. Wilson carrying a huge silver tray. " I hope everybody likes chocolate," she said while Cherry and Lynn passed out napkins. " In our family anything's fine just so it's chocolate."

" Watch it, honey," Mr. Wilson cautioned Lynn as she tripped over Tony's long legs stretched out from the ottoman he had perched on. " This apartment is not much bigger than a cup and saucer. We love having company, but just can't entertain the way we'd like to."

Mr. Adams leaned forward eagerly, and his chubby face broke into a wreath of smiles. " It won't be long till we have our game room in shape for entertaining — then we'll throw a big shindig."

A startling groan came from the corner of the room where Bentley had been slouching in glum silence. His face was flushed and the cut-glass dish tilted on the saucer in his shaking hand.

" Look what you're doing, Bentley! " his mother cried out. " You're going to spill it all over yourself."

Tony's jaw tightened in a surge of sympathy for his friend. Poor Bentley! Why did his father have to bring up the touchy subject of the game room? Why did his mother treat him like a two-year-old baby?

Mr. Wilson rushed to Bentley's rescue just in time to save his trousers from a chocolate bath. " That's all right, young fellow. I never could balance a dish on my knee either," he chuckled. " Lynn, the breakfast nook might be a more comfortable place for you and your friends to have a private conversation. Don't you want to move out? "

The invitation was quickly accepted and, after the move was made, Bentley seemed to relax a little. He watched with interest as Lynn pushed the parakeet cage to one side from the middle of the table.

" Would you like to see my bird? "

With a quick gesture, she removed the flowered covering from the top of the cage. " He probably won't be very lively because he's gone to bed for the night and doesn't like to be disturbed. Do you, Kim? "

She opened the little barred door and stuck in her finger, clicking her tongue invitingly. But the bird refused to budge from his perch. He ruffled his blue feathers and dropped his head sleepily.

" Oh, let him alone," Tony grinned, licking the chocolate from his spoon. " How would you like to be waked up to show off for company? "

" But he's so smart," Lynn replied, closing the door with a resigned sigh. " He can count to ten and he knows lots of tricks like picking up a dime with his beak and tossing it into the air."

Tony lowered his spoon slowly as a brilliant idea took form in his mind. " Say — I think I have a solution to our problem."

" What problem? " Lynn held the flowered cloth motionless as she was about to cover the cage, while she studied Tony's face curiously.

" Don't you remember? " Tony glanced at Bentley but he was busily eating his sundae. " About the next production of the Be Dramatic Club? "

Cherry looked up from her dish, bright-eyed and expectant. " Tony's full of good ideas."

Lynn clapped her hands together softly. " Then tell us. Tell us all about it — quick! "

" Can't." Tony shook his head. " I haven't worked out all the details. You'd better finish your ice cream before it melts."

" I wish you wouldn't be so stubborn," Lynn pouted. But she sat down obediently and picked up her spoon. " When will you tell us? "

" Let's have a meeting in our back yard tomorrow morning. Can everybody be there by ten? I think I'll have something terrific to tell you by that time."

It was agreed to call a meeting for ten o'clock.

3

T ONY WAS UNUSUALLY
quiet at breakfast the next morning. He stirred his
cereal with a brooding, faraway look in his eyes. Across
the table, Cherry tried hard to keep from yawning. Her
sleep had been restless and broken by strange dreams of
flickering lights in dark windows.

"We're not a very lively family this morning," Dad
observed. "Was the night life too strenuous for you?"

"No," Tony said dully. "We had a swell time.
Didn't we, Cherry? Everything was just dandy."

Cherry nodded, but her lips were closed tight as a
clam and the expression on her face was unconvincing.

Their mother seemed to sense that something was
being held back. "If you're thinking about the light in
Captain Gabe's house," she began, "please forget it.
There's not a thing to worry about."

"Oh, it's not that!" Tony was quick to assure her.
"It's about our Dramatic Club."

"I'd almost forgotten your meeting last night." Mrs.

Parker's smile was tender and understanding. " Did Bentley have disturbing news? "

" Not exactly." Tony paused. " But he was pretty upset. We can't have our shows in his basement any more. His mother and dad are planning to fix it up fancy for a recreation room. Naturally, they don't want a lot of kids in there."

Dad's eyebrows lifted quizzically. " Just for grownups, h'm? " He suddenly remembered Mr. Adams' invitation to a shindig and Bentley's unexpected reaction.

" But that's all right." Tony's face began to brighten. " I got to thinking last night that we could give an outdoor show in our back yard. Do you like that idea? "

" Can't think of a better one." Dad glanced at Mother. " Can you, dear? "

" Sounds like a fine plan to me," Mrs. Parker agreed. " Have you told the others? "

" Not yet. " Tony was now grinning happily. " We're going to hold a meeting here this morning, and with your approval I thought I'd suggest a pet show."

Dad threw back his head and laughed heartily, then in a more serious vein said, " It's a good thing your mother likes animals."

" Of course I do. And it's a good thing our yard is fenced in." Her face beamed as she began to see all sorts of interesting possibilities in Tony's idea for a pet show. " I hope you'll let me help."

Mr. Parker pushed back his chair and kissed her lightly on the cheek. " Sounds like this project is off to a good start. You'll have to watch her, though, or she'll be running the whole show," he teased. " And now if I may be excused, it's time to be off to my own job."

Before leaving for his office at the Hillsport Plastic Plant, he slipped on his glasses and stopped at the bulletin board hanging on the kitchen wall and began to read activities for the day. " I see Mother's going to the church luncheon at noon. Cherry and Tony are going to clean up the cellar. Fine! How are Eloise and the kittens getting along? Isn't it about time for you to start finding homes for those little fellows? "

" I've found a place for two of them," Cherry said. " Mrs. Jackson wants to take them to her son's farm next time she's in town. She says the mice are terrible, and she never allowed even one mouse in Captain Gabe's house all the time she was living there."

" Maybe we could keep little Calico Cat," Tony remarked hopefully. " She'd be awful cute for the pet show."

Dad simply looked at him over the rim of his glasses with an expression that might mean yes and might mean no. Then he turned and jotted down another item. " Better fill those birdbaths of Captain Gabe's before you start on the cellar. I noticed they were pretty dry last night."

" We didn't get to show Lynn the carriage house," Cherry remembered. " May we take her along? "

" And Bentley? " Tony added.

" If he wants to go," Cherry mumbled under her breath.

Dad nodded. " Just be sure to do your job up there and get back for the cellar."

" We will," Cherry promised.

" And we'll keep an eye on the place," Tony said stanchly.

After feeding Eloise and the kittens, Tony and Cherry finished their morning chores and began to get ready for the Dramatic Club meeting. They pulled the lawn chairs and rustic table to a shady spot under the apple tree, facing the flower border where a few lazy bees were buzzing around the red and orange zinnias,

the purple asters, and the low edging of dwarf marigolds.

Their mother brought out a pitcher of lemonade and a tray of tall glasses. Tony listened to the tinkling ice appreciatively. " I hope they're on time," he said. " Or I might be tempted to drink that whole pitcherful before they get here, I'm so thirsty."

" Tony — you wouldn't! " Cherry exclaimed as if she believed his threat.

But she didn't have to worry. Lynn and Bentley

came through the picket gate in the hedge just as Mrs. Parker went into the house after stopping to wave to them from the back door.

Lynn's bouncing step broke into a run and she left Bentley straggling behind, looking as if he'd just bitten into a sour apple.

"Tony Parker," she panted, flopping into a chair. "Hurry and get the suspense over. I almost couldn't go to sleep last night wondering what you were going to tell us."

"Well, let's wait for Bentley," Tony said with unperturbed dignity. "Then you can open the meeting any time — you're the president, you know."

Lynn shaded her eyes with her hand as Bentley approached with a bored air. "Have a seat, Mr. Adams," she said, "and we'll consider the meeting open."

Bentley bit his lower lip and sat down. He didn't like the way Lynn was always addressing him as "Mr. Adams." It sounded as though she were making fun of him. But he decided not to make an issue of it just now. He was as anxious to hear Tony's solution to their problem as she was, although he tried not to show it.

Lynn stretched back in her chair with an expectant smile on her lips. "Now we're ready. Begin."

"Well, I thought —" Tony's voice was deliberate and unhurried. "I thought it would be fun to give an outdoor show for a change — right here in our back yard."

Lynn's face fell. "Oh, dear! I hoped you were going to say we could use Captain Gabe's carriage house."

"But, Lynn, you know we can't do that," Cherry said quickly. "Everything on the hill is locked up tight. No one can go in there because no one knows who the property belongs to until the new will turns up."

" Well, why don't they hurry and find it? " Lynn burst out impatiently.

" They've searched the entire place," Tony explained. " And now the lawyers are examining his papers and safe-deposit boxes."

" Maybe Bentley was right about the light last night," Lynn said, sitting bolt upright. " Maybe it was a flashlight he saw and not a reflection at all." She turned to Cherry and gave out a little squeal. " Didn't you say Captain Gabe had a housekeeper who knew something about the will? "

Cherry felt a cold chill creep down her spine. " Yes," she admitted, as if she herself were being accused of trespassing. " But it couldn't have been Mrs. Jackson. She packed all her belongings and went to live in the country with her son right after the funeral."

" But she might have come back last night," Lynn persisted, " and gone snooping through the house trying to find the will."

" Mrs. Jackson wouldn't snoop," Tony bristled. " Besides, she had no personal interest in the new will. She only witnessed it. Dad said Captain Gabe left her a lifetime income in annuities a long time before he left on his trip."

" Mother told us to forget about the light," Cherry said firmly. " There's nothing to worry about."

Bentley placed the tips of his fingers together thoughtfully. " Instead of stewing about a will, why don't we discuss plans for the outdoor show? What did you have in mind, Tony? "

" It was really Lynn who gave me the idea last night," Tony began. " When she said her parakeet could do a lot of tricks, I got to thinking it would be fun to have a pet show. Skippy knows some pretty good tricks too, and Calico Cat would be real cute."

Lynn took up the idea with her usual enthusiasm. " We could invite anyone who has a pet to enter by paying a small entrance fee, and then we could give a prize for the smartest, the most unusual, the prettiest, and the ugliest, or any other division we decided to make."

" Mom loves animals," Cherry put in. " And she'd help us if we wanted her."

" What about me? " Bentley blurted out self-consciously. " I haven't a single, solitary pet. Not even so much as a goldfish."

" I was coming to that," Tony said soothingly. " You'd make a fine master of ceremonies. If you could borrow your dad's silk top hat again, the one you wore in the magic show, you'd look splendiferous and give the whole exhibition an impressive, ceremonious air."

Bentley shook his head with a wry smile. " Not me! The dogs would be acting up, chasing the cats, and the cats would be spitting and sticking out their claws. What a scramble! " Bentley shivered. " Somebody might even bring a snake."

Lynn put her hands on her hips and gave him a baleful stare. " Bentley Adams, I do believe you're afraid of your shadow. Tony comes up with a perfectly wonderful idea and you start throwing cold water on it. You're afraid of everything." A sudden sly gleam came into her eyes. " Aren't you afraid of those bees buzzing around the flowers? Wait a minute. Don't move. One of them lighted on your head."

Tony and Cherry, feeling ill at ease, glanced at Bentley, but there was no sign of a bee disturbing his neatly combed hair.

" Just sit still," Lynn went on teasing him. " Maybe it'll fly away without stinging you."

Bentley's face twitched and his neck was held stiff as a stick. Tony was about to tell Lynn to cut out the comedy, when Bentley jumped to his feet and looked wildly from one to the other. " This may be very amusing for you but not for me," he shouted. " You can give any kind of show you want to, but you can give it without me. I'm going home! "

All three watched with dismay as Bentley strode across the grass and through the gate, leaving it standing wide open behind him.

Cherry was first to break the stunned silence. " Something must be bothering Bentley. He never leaves the gate open."

Tony laughed shortly. " I guess so. And I can't say I blame him for leaving in such a hurry."

" I didn't mean to make him mad." Lynn was almost tearful. " I'll run after him and tell him I'm sorry."

She was on her feet in an instant, but Tony held her back.

" No. Don't go now. Give him time to cool off. In fact, it might be better not to mention it at all."

" But I *am* sorry," Lynn insisted. " Bentley is your friend and Cherry's, and I don't want him to be mad at you."

38

Tony smacked his knee smartly. "I'll tell you what let's do. We'll take the water up the hill to the bird-baths and on the way we'll stop and invite him to go along. Bentley never holds a grudge."

After bringing two buckets up from the cellar, Tony told his mother they were getting ready to leave. Cherry and Lynn helped him get water from the outdoor hydrant with only a few splashes on their blue jeans and on Skipper, who had waked up from a nap and persisted in trying to help too. The buckets were loaded on Tony's old red wagon, which was still sturdy after many years of use and often came in handy for the long pull up the hill.

Skipper pranced along beside the turning wheels as they rattled along the sidewalk. After turning the corner, they came in sight of Bentley sitting in the swing under the oak tree in his own front yard. The swing was moving ever so slightly and Bentley's shoulders were hunched in an attitude of utter dejection.

Tony turned the wagon handle over to Cherry and ran forward smiling eagerly. "D'you want to help me pull the wagon up the hill?"

"I don't see why you want me," Bentley protested. "You and Cherry and Lynn can go up there by yourselves."

Tony shrugged, still smiling. "You don't have to go. It's our job, Cherry's and mine. We promised to show Lynn the carriage house."

"And we want you to go to," Lynn pleaded, coming up behind Tony. "We really do."

Bentley gave her a stony look and then his face relaxed. "I guess it won't take long to fill those birdbaths and then we can come back here and finish our meeting about the pet show."

When Cherry saw them coming back together, she gave an energetic tug at the wagon and waves of water splashed over the brim of each bucket.

" Wait a minute," Bentley called out. " You're getting all wet. I've read that if you drop in a piece of wood or something that will float, the water won't slosh over."

He looked around earnestly, and his face lighted up at sight of Skipper dragging a small branch that had fallen from the oak tree. " Here, Skippy. Drop it. That's just the thing." He broke off two pieces of the branch about six inches long and dropped one into each bucket.

" Now if you don't object, I'll help Tony pull the wagon," he smiled, releasing Cherry's fingers from the handle.

With Tony and Bentley in front, Cherry fell back to walk with Lynn, whose bouncing step lengthened to keep up the swift pace set by the boys. They both felt good again and burst out laughing at Skipper, dancing up and down beside the wagon trying to discover what had become of his plaything.

At the top of the hill, when they had left the driveway to walk through the garden, the tall, tangled grass made the going rough. The girls tried to help by pushing the back of the wagon. Two blue jays, flying from one tree to another, screeched shrill cries of alarm.

Tony squinted upward as the wagon came to a halt beside a shaded birdbath. " We're just bringing you some water. Is that any way to say ' thank you '? "

"Maybe they're fussing at Skippy," Bentley suggested. "Maybe they don't want him around."

"Skipper has as much right here as they have," Tony grinned. "Wasn't he Captain Gabe's own dog? Wasn't this his home?"

"It's an awful gruesome-looking home," Bentley said, with a nervous glance at the second floor where the light had flashed from a front window the night before. "Wild horses couldn't drag me in there."

"I doubt if you could get in even with wild horses to help you." Tony's voice was matter-of-fact. "It's locked up safe and sound."

They moved on to the second birdbath, and Tony poured water into the blue bowl after Cherry had removed bits of twig and dry leaves.

Lynn stood with her back to the others, taking in every detail of the low, rambling building, which showed mellow old brick through the heavy growth of vines. So this was the carriage house! She wondered what it was like inside. There were no windows on the side visible to her gaze, and the heavy faded-green door looked forbidding.

She whirled around suddenly, her eyes dancing. "What a keen place to give our shows! If George ever comes back, I hope he gets this property and lets us use it. I'd sure like to take a look inside that carriage house. Why don't we try the door?"

Tony tramped through the tall grass and turned the knob of the solid wooden door. "Locked," he called back, "just as I told you."

"Come on. Let's go home," Bentley said crossly. "We haven't got all day to stick around here."

"I know what's in there anyway," Cherry said, scarcely noticing Bentley's uneasiness. "There are stalls in one wing for several horses and Captain Gabe's cars where the carriages used to be kept. There's really not much to see." She turned abruptly. "Wonder what Skippy's barking about."

"Probably chasing a squirrel," Tony smiled. "Sounds like he's barking on the other side of the house."

Tony was right. Just then a large gray squirrel shot around the corner, with Skippy close on his trail. Quick as a flash, the squirrel ran beneath the bushes along the side of the house and disappeared down the deep areaway of a basement window. Skippy went right after him.

"He's cornered!" Tony shouted and, dashing ahead of the others, squeezed between the tall mock orange bushes.

When Cherry, Lynn, and Bentley reached the spot, Tony's startled face appeared through the leaves. "They're both gone," he gasped. "Right through an open window!"

CHAPTER

4

As TONY PUSHED THE branches of the bush aside the other three crowded in with him around the brick areaway. When they peered down, there was no sign of Skipper and no sign of the large gray squirrel.

Tony pointed dramatically to the open window leading into the basement. " I don't know how this could have happened, but they've both disappeared."

" Just like the White Rabbit in *Alice in Wonderland!* " Lynn exclaimed.

" Well, what d'you know! " Bentley breathed heavily.

" We'll have to go right in there and get them out immediately." Cherry's voice was full of anxiety. " They'll be tearing around like mad, upsetting everything and making a terrible mess."

She dropped to her knees and stared down the cool brick sides of the areaway. " It's a pretty far drop, but I think I can make it."

Bentley's face turned pale. " You're not going inside, surely? "

" Of course. There's nothing else we can do." Cherry looked at his alarmed face in mild surprise. " You know Skippy can't jump out by himself."

" Here, let me go first," Tony said. In a twinkling, he scrambled over the brick ledge and jumped down, landing on his feet with a light thud. " See! No trick at all. And it's not over my head."

" But it'll be over your head, Cherry," Bentley warned.

Without heeding the warning, Cherry flipped over from her knees to her stomach and slid feet first into the dark hole, just as Tony ducked through the window and dropped to the basement floor. Cherry followed close behind him.

Left alone on the outside, Lynn turned to Bentley. " Come on. Don't you want to help? " She studied him through narrowed eyes. " We're not afraid, are we? "

Bentley hesitated, shifting uneasily from one foot to the other. Suddenly his lips flattened into a straight line. " It's your turn — go on. Then get out of my way."

Lynn moved rapidly and Bentley dropped after her, landing on one foot and one knee. He stood up quickly and brushed the dust from his jeans while the others were gazing around.

The basement seemed enormous, with the solemn stillness of an empty cave. The huge old furnace was like a fat octopus with writhing tentacles stretching in all directions. There was a cot near the boiler and a wooden table with three weather-beaten captain's

45

chairs drawn up. On the table was an empty Coke bottle and a paper plate holding a scrap of hamburger bun and a few soggy rings of onion slices.

Tony walked to the table and gingerly poked the morsel of bun. " H'm. Looks like somebody's been having a lunch." He thought it better not to mention that the bun felt a little fresh. No use alarming anyone.

" Guess they didn't like onions," Cherry observed with her funny little twist of humor.

Bentley let out a sudden wail. " I'm going to get out of here."

" We're all going to get out," Cherry said, her eyes roving about the room, " as soon as we find Skippy and the squirrel."

" Now where can that dog be? " Tony muttered, running behind the furnace.

Lynn and Cherry circled the walls, one going to the right and one to the left, peering behind boxes and along shelves, although it didn't seem likely that a squirrel or a dog could be concealed without making a sound.

Bentley waited nervously in the middle of the floor until the other three had completed their rounds.

" Listen," Cherry whispered. " Do you hear anything? "

No sound could be heard in the big house. Only the chirping and twittering of birds came to their ears through the open window.

" I'll bet he chased that squirrel up the steps," Tony said, pounding his fist into his open palm. He rushed toward the stairway. " We'll have to go up and see."

" I'm not going with you," Bentley announced flatly.

46

Running toward the window, he reached for the sill, which was an inch or two above his hand.

"You can't get out that way," Tony said with weary patience. "As soon as we find Skippy and the squirrel we can all go out the back door. It has a night lock that opens from the inside."

Bentley gave in and stumbled up the steps after the others with a pounding heart. Before they reached the top step, they could hear the click of Skipper's toenails on the bare hall floor. It was not the sound of swift pursuit but a slow, tired drag.

As they pressed through the narrow doorway, Skipper greeted them by dropping to the floor flat on his tummy. His tongue was hanging out as he panted with exhaustion, a foolish grin pulling back the corners of his mouth.

"What's the matter, boy?" Tony laughed. "Did you lose that squirrel?"

"Oh, dear," Cherry murmured. "We simply *can't* leave a squirrel in Captain Gabe's house. He might chew up something." She glanced up and down the hall, a worried pucker creasing her forehead.

"He must be up toward the front," Lynn suggested. "Skippy came from that direction."

"Sure he did!" Tony exclaimed. "His tail's pointing that way now."

"O.K." Cherry said briskly. "Please put Skipper out the back door, Tony, and let's hunt for the squirrel."

Tony picked up the tired dog and carried him down the hall with Bentley tagging along behind him to open the door. After he had released the night lock, Tony thrust the dog out on the back steps and slammed the door before Bentley could mention leaving.

While they were waiting, Lynn's attention was caught by an array of bells suspended from the ceiling along the east wall of the dimly lighted corridor.

" What are those bells for? " she asked Cherry while Tony was trying the knob to be sure the door was locked.

" They came from Captain Gabe's boat, an old-time stern-wheeler named the *Edna M.*"

Tony came running back, full of animation. " He told us all about the meaning of the bells and how he rigged them up here just like they were on his boat."

" Modern boats have diesel air horns," Bentley said, coming up behind him.

" But these bells are much prettier sounding and each one has a different tone," Cherry went on.

" You see, each one has a meaning," Tony explained. " A series of brass rings and wooden handles in the pilothouse was attached to a clothesline, which ran over a lot of little wheels down in the engine room. It was a long way, and they were connected to the bells hanging from the ceiling of the engine room — all sizes of bells."

" One is even a cowbell," Cherry giggled.

Lynn listened with wide-eyed interest as Tony continued: " If your boat was going full speed ahead and you wanted to slow up, you pulled the backing bell one time for slow. Then you rang the cowbell for dead slow. If you wanted to go from dead slow to half speed, you rang a gong. There's a bigger gong for full speed."

" Captain Gabe used to let us ring them," Cherry said proudly. " He loved to hear them because they re-

48

minded him of his boat. Only, they meant different things here. There's a brass ring by the front door. It's attached by a pulley to that biggest bell and it ding-dongs through the house when someone pulls the brass ring. There's another one for the back door and one for each room in the house."

Bentley seemed more at ease as he became interested in the story of the bells. For the moment, they had all forgotten about the squirrel.

" Imagine putting a system like that in your house! " Bentley shook his head slowly. " Everybody said he was a queer old codger."

Cherry's face flushed with indignation. " He was not! Just because he had a pink bald head and white whiskers, you don't have to call him old. And he wasn't any of those other things, either."

" It doesn't matter," Lynn said soothingly. " It all sounds very interesting to me. Tell us more about the bells, Tony."

" Well, I think the most interesting one of all is on top of the carriage house. It's the biggest, too." He rounded his arms to show the impressive size. " It used to be on the top deck of the boat. Captain Gabe said that when they were casting that bell, he threw in a hundred Mexican dollars to melt in the bell metal."

" That was to make the tone more beautiful," Cherry said, forgetting all about her flare-up at Bentley.

Lynn's eyes sparkled. " Wouldn't it be slick to ring a bell like that for people to come to our shows in the carriage house! "

" Everybody could hear it all right, all right," Tony chuckled. " Captain Gabe used to ring that big bell for George to come home when he was a younger boy out playing. He said you could hear it anyplace in this part of town — clear down to the river even."

" They gave shows on some of the boats a long time ago," Cherry said enthusiastically. " There were regular showboats that stopped at each town along the river. But Captain Gabe's boat was a packet that carried passengers and mail and freight."

Bentley was growing restless again. " Hadn't we better find that squirrel and get out of here? We can't use the carriage house so we'd better finish our meeting and decide what to do."

" That's right," Tony agreed with a good-natured smile. " Cherry, where would you hide if you were a squirrel? "

Cherry wrinkled her nose impishly. " I'd jump in a hollow stump."

" Well, there's none here," Tony grinned, and started toward the front of the house.

They all filed after him into the dining room on their left, the high ceiling and heavily curtained windows giving it a formal and dignified appearance. The beautifully polished oak paneling on the walls was much too smooth for a squirrel to climb. A thorough search around the room revealed no likely hiding place and there was not a single clue to the animal's whereabouts.

" No stumps in here," Tony said gaily, and darted across the hall to the softly carpeted living room. At first they could hardly see anything, for the curtains were drawn at the windows front and back and at the two on either side of the wide fireplace.

" That's George's grand piano," Cherry whispered

51

to Lynn as a feeling almost of awe crept over her.

Tony walked around a sheet-covered chair. " I'll look inside." He stretched out his hands and frowned. " I guess I won't. The keyboard's locked."

" He probably didn't want any dust to get inside," Cherry said. " But the top sure is dusty."

Tony grew reminiscent as his eyes gazed at the mellow wood. " George loved that piano as much as Captain Gabe loved his boat."

Cherry tilted her head upward. " Maybe the squirrel is hiding up there." She pointed to the crystal chandelier hung with myriad cut-glass prisms.

" Isn't that a beauty! " Lynn exclaimed. " Captain Gabe must have been a very wealthy man."

Cherry nodded. " My dad said he was one of the richest river boat captains."

" He did his own buying and selling," Tony explained. " Instead of just hauling for other people, he'd buy anything that was for sale. Sometimes he'd buy a load of cattle from a farmer along the way and take them down the river to sell, all bawling and milling around on his boat. In the fall, he bought barrels of apples from the orchards near the riverbanks and took them to market."

" Wonder where he got that chandelier? " Lynn mused, still lost in admiration.

" That was on the *Edna M.,*" Cherry replied, " in a beautiful room called the Plush Cabin. He brought it home when the boat was dismantled."

" Look," Bentley interrupted. " There's a picture of George on the mantel. See how good-looking he is in a uniform."

Lynn walked closer. " Hope I can meet him in person someday."

Tony, who was scouting around the room looking under the chairs and behind every piece of furniture, turned abruptly. " Hey! Listen to Skipper barking out there. He's not chasing squirrels now. That's the way he barks when someone comes to the door."

" If someone is at the back door," Cherry piped up, " why doesn't he ring the bell? " She spoke as if it were the most natural thing in the world for a visitor to come acalling at a house long unoccupied.

Skippy's staccato barking dwindled down to a few gruff growls.

" Just keep still," Lynn whispered. " Maybe whoever it is will go away."

Tony made a move toward the hall and Bentley clutched at his arm. " What are you planning to do? " he demanded frantically.

" I'm going to see who it is," Tony replied, drawing away from Bentley's shaking hand.

The sound of his feet on the bare hall floor echoed dully as he rounded the stairway and disappeared from view. Waiting tensely, they heard his footsteps falter, then stop. In a few seconds, which seemed to them like dragging minutes, his scampering feet were coming back. The broad grin on his face was reassuring.

" Nobody there," he announced. " Except Skippy. He's lying over by the carriage house wagging his tail."

" Do you suppose," Lynn asked eagerly, " that somebody went into the carriage house? "

Bentley was scornful. " That's impossible," he snapped. " You know very well the door is locked. Tony

53

couldn't budge it. And what's more, we'll never find that squirrel if you stand here talking all day."

" That's right," Tony agreed. " But it's a cinch he's not down here. We'll have to go upstairs and look."

" We'll hurry," Cherry promised, glancing at Bentley, who looked grim but resigned.

As they started up the winding stairway, Tony's face glowed with a joyful memory. " Captain Gabe always let me slide down the banister. He'd yell, ' Ring your bell, son, when you come around that bend.' Gee, it was fun! Just like flying."

He ran ahead of the others and threw his leg over the banister at the top of the stairs.

" You'd better not," Cherry cautioned, running after him. " The railing's covered with dust! "

Tony chuckled. " I'll clean it off — but good."

Bentley and Lynn reached the top of the stairs just as Tony pushed off.

" Whee! " he yelled. " Watch me go! "

As he rounded the curve, the loud peal of a bell filled the farthest corners of the house. Tony stopped with a jerk at the newel post and bounded back up the steps, two at a time, to join the frozen-faced group on the top landing.

" That was the f-f-front doorbell! " he stammered. " It's the loudest one on the line."

CHAPTER

5

THE SILENT SECONDS
dragged by and then it came again, an insistent tug of
the brass ring outside the front door, spilling an un-
canny sound throughout the lonely house. The weird
echoes of the bell closed about the huddled group at
the top of the stairs.

Tony straightened his shoulders and laughed softly.
He tried to sound as unconcerned as possible. " How
silly! " he said in an offhand manner. " There's nothing to be afraid of. Here it is broad daylight; somebody
rings the doorbell and we all jump like scared rabbits."

" Why shouldn't we? " Bentley retorted. " We have
no business being in this house at all. We're — we're
trespassers, that's what we are."

Lynn immediately rose to their defense. " How d'you
like that! We came in just to protect this property and
you know it."

While Lynn was talking, Tony moved with resolute
feet along the deep carpeting of the upper hall and

peered through the French doors leading to the balcony that stretched across the second story of the house. Glimpses of the river were visible through the treetops, but everything directly below was hidden from view.

" I can't see over the railing from here," he muttered, his hand on the knob. " If there were some way I could open this door — "

As he twisted the glass knob, the door opened as if a magic word had broken an enchanted spell. Tony slipped out noiselessly and tiptoed across the balcony while the others watched breathlessly from the doorway.

Of course there was nothing to be afraid of, but there was something just a little mysterious about the bell ringing in a closed-up house. They waited tensely as he tiptoed back and closed the door behind him.

" Just as I thought. It was a perfectly innocent man — a blind man," he explained reassuringly. " He must have been one of those peddlers going from house to house, because he had a basket of pins and needles and stuff like that. Of course he didn't know that nobody lives here. He was just leaving." Breaking off his words, he turned and looked over his shoulder. " See — there he is going down the driveway, tapping with his cane."

" It's a good thing Skipper wasn't out front," Bentley said. " He might have scared the poor fellow half to death, barking like he was going to chew off a leg."

" You know Skipper wouldn't hurt him," Cherry protested. " He wouldn't hurt anybody. As soon as a stranger speaks to him, he gets all waggly-tail and friendly. He just likes to pretend he's a watchdog."

Lynn laughed with relief as the feeling of fright wore

56

off. "We act like a bunch of sissies when it's nothing but imagination working overtime."

Bentley pointed to the door with a dramatic gesture. "Imagination! You may call it that, but I'd like to know why that door opened when everything is supposed to be locked tight. Do you think that was imagination?"

The others exchanged puzzled glances without answering.

Bentley pressed his point farther as he saw he was at last gaining their respectful attention. "And that window in the basement. Did we just imagine it was unlocked?" His voice rose higher and higher. "I know good and well that somebody's been in here and the sooner we get out the better."

Tony shrugged his shoulders. "Don't get so excited. We've got a job to do, and we're going to find that squirrel if we possibly can and then we'll go." He motioned with his head toward the open door across the hall. "Let's look in Captain Gabe's study."

Bentley swallowed his objections when he saw that the others seemed eager to follow. There was at least safety in numbers, and he had no intention of going back alone.

Lynn was thrilled at the prospect of going inside the room that had looked so interesting the night before when she glimpsed it briefly from the hall. She had hoped for a chance to return, and now it was happening much sooner than she had expected.

When they entered the room, she suddenly remembered something significant with a walloping jolt. Last night, when she had been admiring the desk with its rich carving as it caught the last fleeting movement of the flashlight, Mr. Parker had closed the study door. She remembered her disappointment and her desire to come back and examine the boat model. She remembered the definite click of the latch. Now that door was standing open!

Surely she remembered correctly, although Tony and Cherry didn't seem to notice anything unusual as they walked in. The door had been shut when they left, she was positive, but she decided not to mention it now — not where Bentley could hear. He might start objecting again and insist on leaving before they found the squirrel or even had a peek at the room.

Right now, his objections seemed to be forgotten as he stared around the study which Captain Gabe called his " cabin." Although Bentley had been a visitor in the house, he had never been in the " cabin " before. Only Cherry and Tony had been privileged to enter the Captain's private quarters.

A huge anchor took up most of one entire wall. It had once been on the *Edna M.,* and for years the great gilded anchor swung jauntily between her smokestacks.

The other walls were hung with pictures of river boats: stern-wheelers and side-wheelers, towboats, and excursion boats. There were framed photographs of Captain Gabe's friends, both captains and crew men. They were an old-fashioned-looking lot of men with flowing beards or bushy black mustaches.

Looking at the pictures, Lynn cocked her head to one side. " He sure knew a lot of people." She waved her arm in a wide sweep. " Are these all friends of his? "

Cherry nodded. " Captain Gabe never met a stran-

58

ger," she replied proudly. " He made friends with everybody wherever he happened to be. He was very talkative and loved to swap stories."

" He told us some awful good stories," Tony put in eagerly. " Here's a picture of a wooden stern-wheeler he told us about. It got grounded in a cornfield one night during a flood. The pilot was navigating in the dark and pretty soon he was lost. The water was falling at the time and his boat got stuck. They had to wait till the rain started coming down again and the river could rise high enough to carry the boat on her way." He pointed to the details of the picture. " See how twisted she is."

He stepped back for Bentley and Lynn to have a closer look. " But she got straightened out," he added, imitating Captain Gabe's chuckle. " Then she went back to business."

Lynn soon moved on to the other side of the room, to the old-fashioned desk that stood near the window. Her eyes roved over the intricate model of the river boat that had caught her attention the night before.

" Isn't she a dandy! " Tony said as he and Bentley joined Lynn. " That's an exact copy of Captain Gabe's boat, the *Edna M.*"

" It was named for his wife," Cherry piped up helpfully.

" The original *Edna M.* boat has never been sold," Tony went on. " It's at the wharf in a quiet spot up the river, waiting to be disposed of."

" Gee, I'd like to see it," Lynn sighed.

Tony waved his hand. " It looks just like this. See the little pilothouse on top and all those little bitty windows opening on the decks."

" Maybe the squirrel is hiding in there," Cherry said with twinkling eyes. " It's about the right size, and if I were a squirrel, I'd like to get inside there."

Bentley studied the model curiously. " I don't see how a squirrel could get in through those tiny windows."

" I guess not," Tony laughed. " We'd better start looking for that hollow stump Cherry was talking about."

He dropped down on his hands and knees and began running his fingers back and forth beneath the desk. " I can't see him and I can't feel him, so I guess he's not hiding under here."

" Oh, look! " Cherry said suddenly, pointing to a picture on the desk of a chubby little boy in uniform. " That's George. It was made a long time ago. Captain Gabe said that when he bought him that captain's suit George was so proud he almost busted his buttons."

Lynn clasped her hands behind her back and smiled at the handsome child in the picture. " I'm sure he had reason to be proud. Look at that double-breasted suit with four brass buttons down each side. I'd like to see him in the uniform he's wearing now."

Tony looked up from the floor and grinned. " Not much chance when he's a thousand miles away. You and Cherry had better quit gabbing so much and get busy or we'll never find the squirrel."

Bently was still admiring the *Edna M*. " Come here a minute, Tony," he said. " This boat is keen! Look at the workmanship on that paddle wheel. Who made it? "

" An old man up at the wharf — name of Mr. Bing-

60

ham. He was a friend of Captain Gabe's and almost as interesting as the Captain." Tony stood up and began a rapid flow of words. " Notice that gangplank. Real pulleys too. And these twin smokestacks. Just like the real boat."

Bentley smiled wryly. " Next you'll be telling us real smoke comes out there."

Leaving the boys to their conversation, the two girls began a businesslike search around the room, looking under chairs and turning over cushions. As they moved about, Cherry smiled and whispered to Lynn, " Now look who's doing the gabbing! "

Lynn wrinkled her nose. " Oh, well, at least the boat has made Bentley forget his fears."

" What's inside of it? " he wanted to know next.

Tony hesitated. " Nothing, I s'pose. Just hollow."

Bentley gave him a sidelong glance. " You're sure there's not a crystal chandelier? " He leaned forward and squinted through one of the tiny windows. " No — I guess you're right. Just hollow."

" I'm getting kind of hollow myself," Tony said, rubbing his stomach. " Isn't it about lunch time? "

" But we haven't found the squirrel," Cherry wailed. " Lunch time or not, we've got to find him." She replaced a cushion. " One thing's certain — he's not in here."

Bentley was still studying the carved desk intently. " You know what? " he said, stepping back. " If anyone wanted to hide a will, this desk would be a good place."

" This whole house has been searched for the will," Cherry informed him, with a slight edge of disapproval

62

n her voice. " Anyway, we're hunting for a squirrel. Let's go on to the rest of the upstairs."

As they moved toward the door, they were frozen in their tracks by the lively gong of a bell in the very room where they stood. All eyes were fixed on the small, graceful bell that hung above the door, mounted on a block of dark, polished wood. They couldn't believe their ears, but the small clapper seemed to quiver as the sound faded away.

" Someone's downstairs," Cherry whispered in a shaky voice.

Bentley gave a low moan and a rising panic spread through their minds. Who could have rung the bell, and what reason did he have for ringing it?

Tony was the first to move. " Come on," he said firmly. " I know a way out."

Like a flock of birds startled into sudden flight, there was a streak of movement into the hall as they followed Tony toward the door leading to the balcony.

" Thank goodness it was unlocked," Lynn panted as Tony softly closed the French doors behind them.

Bentley, weak in the knees, leaned against the strong column for support, pale-faced and shaking.

" Wh-wh-what do we do now? " he quavered.

" Just follow me," Tony ordered, striding across the balcony. " I've done this before and it's easy."

Quicker than they could say " scat," he was over the railing with both legs wrapped around the column, his arms firmly grasping the smooth white roundness. A swift slide landed him expertly on the porch below. He jumped to the ground and stepped back to give further directions.

" All right, Cherry. You help Lynn over the railing."
A half-smile curved his lips as Lynn's legs dangled awkwardly, trying to find a foothold. " It's a good thing you both wore blue jeans," he chuckled. " Makes the sliding easier."

Once she had got a firm grasp, Lynn's face lost its grimness and she seemed to be enjoying herself. After swooping downward, she was soon standing safe on the ground with Tony.

Gazing upward, they saw that the two on the balcony were having some difficulty. Cherry was talking in muffled tones and tugging at Bentley's arm, which was drawn away forcibly.

" I never saw anything like it," Lynn muttered. " He didn't want to go in and now she can't get him to leave."

Before Tony could think of a persuasive word, there must have been another peal of the bell or some movement from inside. Cherry dropped Bentley's arm, and they both glanced backward and grabbed for the railing.

Cherry was the first one over and slid down with graceful ease. Bentley was so close behind that he almost landed on her shoulders.

Without pausing for words, the four started running down the hill at breakneck speed and did not stop until they reached the oak tree in Bentley's front yard.

Skipper greeted them joyfully, tossing another branch he'd found to play with.

Tony stooped to stroke his head. " How'd you get here, Skipper? "

" Why didn't you wait for us? " Cherry demanded. " Did someone send you home? "

64

CHAPTER
6

THERE WAS NO CHANCE
to discuss the mysterious bell-ringing after their hasty
dash down the hill. Before any one of them could guess
at the cause or express an opinion, Bentley's mother
pushed open the screen door.

" You'd better come in immediately, Son, and get
cleaned up," she called out. " You know you have a
piano lesson this afternoon, and you barely have time
to eat your lunch and get there on the hour."

Bentley glanced toward the porch and nodded ab-
sent-mindedly. Then he turned back with a weary sigh.
" See you later," he murmured and dragged himself
into the house.

Lynn clapped her hand over her mouth as if she
suddenly remembered something important that she
had almost forgotten completely. " Am I a dope! "
she exclaimed. " I almost forgot that Mimi was going to
fix a picnic lunch today. She likes to get out of the apartment, and we were planning to drive around exploring
the countryside with Dad, since we're still new to Hills-

port." She began to run backward in short bouncy steps. " Sorry I have to rush."

After waving good-by, Tony and Cherry walked home in silence with a burning question in their minds — a question neither one was quite ready to put into words.

Deep in their own thoughts, they were surprised to find that their mother had already left the house. But they found a note on the bulletin board in the kitchen, which said:

Gone to church luncheon
Sandwiches and milk in the refrigerator
Don't forget to clean the cellar
Love, Mother

" I guess she couldn't wait," Tony observed glumly. " But I sure wanted to talk to her."

" Should we tell Mom and Dad? "

" Of course," Tony said, his lips in a grim line. " This may be more serious than you realize."

" But you know what will happen if we do," Cherry persisted. " Dad will laugh and say we're being a little bit too dramatic, the way he loves to tease us about the Be Dramatic Club. And Mother will probably say we can't go up there any more. Maybe they won't believe us, or they'll think we're exaggerating."

" Oh, sure, they'll believe us," Tony said with conviction. " And Dad won't laugh. They'll both be able to tell us the right thing to do."

" Well, let's wash our hands and eat," Cherry said briskly. " You get down the glasses for me, please, and I'll get out the sandwiches and milk."

66

Tony began to cheer up as his sister walked toward the refrigerator. The prospect of food was always consoling.

He reached into the cupboard shelf, then whirled around with a glass in each hand. " Who do you think rang that bell in Captain Gabe's cabin? " he burst out, as if the question had been nagging him as long as he could stand it.

" I wish I knew," Cherry replied, pulling up a chair.

" It also worries me," Tony went on, " that we didn't find the squirrel."

Cherry smiled brightly. " Maybe *he* rang the bell! "

" Fat chance," Tony muttered, biting into a sandwich. " But we can't do anything about it right now."

After they finished their lunch, they cleared the table and washed up the dishes they'd used. Tony hung up the damp dish towel, his mind still grappling with the puzzle.

" Are you ready to start cleaning the cellar? " he asked. Maybe tackling the job would help throw off his disturbing thoughts. " We want to have it done when Dad gets home."

" Sure," Cherry agreed. " Wait till I get some milk for the kittens."

The small cellar was dim and shadowy until they switched on the light. Eloise, from her bed in the corner, looked over one black-and-white shoulder and yawned lazily as her three kittens came bounding to the foot of the steps.

The black-and-white one that looked like Eloise came from behind the furnace. The solid black one they called Midnight dropped from the top of the kindling pile, and the little calico-colored favorite leaped from a high shelf where the jars of fruit and vegetables were stored.

" Look at that! " Tony chortled. " I do believe she's going to be an aerial artist, the star performer in our pet show."

Cherry placed the blue bowl of milk on the concrete floor and smiled as three little pink tongues lapped greedily. " Maybe so, but all she thinks about now is eating. Look at the milk on her whiskers! Not very glamorous for a star performer, if you ask me."

Tony glanced at the droplets of milk flying merrily. " This place sure need a good cleaning," he said, and wrinkled his freckled nose. " Smells like spilled milk."

" Remember Dad's old saying," Cherry told him. " ' Never cry over spilled milk.' While you drag down the hose, I'll get the broom, and we'll soon have everything spick-and-span."

Cherry picked up the empty bowl and the piece of worn blanket that served as a bed for the kittens and their mother. Following Tony up the steps, she took it outdoors and spread it on the grass. The sun and air would make it smell clean and sweet again.

When they came back with the broom and hose, they started on the job in high spirits. At the sound of the faucet being turned on, Eloise arose and walked up the steps with an air of dignified disapproval. At the sound of the squirting water, the three kittens stopped licking their whiskers and scampered to the highest shelf, where they hid behind a row of canned peaches. From their safe perch, they watched the entire proceeding with wide-eyed curiosity.

68

Later, as Tony and Cherry rested on the bottom step, discussing Captain Gabe and the house on the hill, the floor began to dry off in spots. Cherry decided it was time to bring the bed blanket from the back yard.

When she came down again, folding it neatly to the right size, Tony was still sitting on the bottom step cuddling Calico Cat.

"You know what?" he said thoughtfully. "It still smells like kittens in here, but it's kind of a nice, cozy smell. Everybody's house has a different smell, I guess. Lynn's house smells like chocolate fudge, and Bentley's house smells like furniture polish."

"And our house smells like kittens," Cherry giggled.

"Yes, and Captain Gabe's house smells haunted," Tony went on.

Cherry's eyes grew round as saucers. "Do you think it might have been a ghost that rang the bell?"

"Oh, Cherry, what a crazy idea," Tony frowned. "You know there aren't any ghosts, except pretend ones on Halloween. That wasn't a ghost ringing the bell, not even a pretend one."

"But it might have been the squirrel, and I'll be glad when we can go back and find out." Cherry wagged her head solemnly. "We'll never get Bentley to go back. But I don't think we even want him. He's a stick-in-the-mud, that's all."

"Don't be so hard on him," Tony said quickly. "We never really know how people feel deep down inside. Maybe something is troubling him and that's why he acts so irritating at times. That's what Mom says, and I think Bentley is just upset because the Dramatic Club can't meet in his basement any more."

" Then we ought to be specially nice to him." Cherry smoothed the blankets as if she would like to smooth away all the troubles in the world.

" Sure. That's right," Tony agreed. " How would you feel if your mother never made chocolate fudge sundaes for your friends like Lynn's mother does? And never let you have pets like our mother does? Bentley doesn't even have a goldfish to tell his troubles to."

" Maybe we ought to give him one of our kittens," Cherry suggested in a warm surge of sympathy. " Let's take one over right now. I bet she'd let him have one of ours."

" Bet she wouldn't."

" You could talk her into it." Cherry's eyes began to sparkle as she rushed over to Tony and put both hands on his shoulders. " You're a good explainer. Then when we have the pet show, Lynn would have a parakeet, we've got Skipper, and Bentley would have a kitten."

Tony seemed to be giving the idea some thought before he answered. " It's worth a try," he said finally. " Which one shall we give him? "

They both looked down at Calico Cat purring peacefully on Tony's knee. She was their favorite. Black and white like Eloise with cinnamon spots for trimming, she was the prettiest one of them all. She was the smartest one too.

Tony raised troubled eyes to Cherry's face. Would it have to be Calico Cat? Wouldn't one of the others do just as well? He couldn't bear to ask it aloud.

But Cherry read his thoughts as she often did. " We'd want to give Bentley the best, wouldn't we? " she asked gently. " Don't you think he'd be good to her? "

" Of course he would," Tony said dismally.

" Then don't worry, Tony. You know Dad said we'd have to find homes for all of them, and if Bentley had Calico Cat, we could see her every day."

Tony picked up the sleepy kitten and curled her in the crook of his arm. " Well, if Bentley's home from his music lesson, let's go."

Cherry followed Tony as he walked slowly up the stairs. " It was almost three by the kitchen clock when I went up for the blanket," she told him, " so he should be home by now."

When the back door closed behind them, Cherry started toward the gate in the hedge, but Tony held her back. He stood there hesitant, clutching the kitten to the front of his striped T-shirt.

" Let's not cut through," he said finally. " Let's go the long way round."

Cherry nodded. Poor Tony, she thought. I can read his mind like a book. He just can't bear to part with Calico Cat, and he wants to put it off as long as possible. But he's being noble about it.

That was partly true. But Tony also needed more time to think about what he would say to Mrs. Adams. How could he best persuade her to accept a pet for Bentley? He kept mulling the question over in his mind as they walked side by side in silence.

When Cherry pushed the front door button, Tony wore a grim but heroic smile. His mind was made up.

Mrs. Adams came to the door and looked at the kitten questioningly. " Bentley isn't home yet," she began.

" But we came to see you," Tony said with his most endearing smile.

"How nice," Mrs. Adams said vaguely. Then she opened the door and let them in. With a puzzled expression she ushered them into the tidy living room, and was offering them seats when Bentley came in the front door with his music rolled under his arm.

"Hi there," Tony greeted him breezily, pretending not to notice the surprise written on his face. "We really came to see your mother, but I guess you'd like to hear what we have to say."

Bentley and his mother both looked so astonished by this unusual announcement that Cherry had to choke back a giggle. Tony gave her a warning glance, and when the others were comfortably seated, he chose a straight-backed chair and perched gingerly on the edge of the seat.

"We were thinking," he began, "of using our back yard for the Be Dramatic Club to give an outdoor show — a pet show." He paused and leaned forward confidentially. "Don't you think that would be nice, Mrs. Adams?"

"I certainly do," she agreed quickly. "The outdoors is a splendid place for a pet show — any kind of show."

"Now, Lynn Wilson has a parakeet to enter," Tony went on evenly, "and we have Skippy and several very nice kittens." He gave Mrs. Adams a sunny smile. "A kitten is one of the cleanest pets in the world, Mrs. Adams. They're always washing themselves. One of the quietest pets too — not always barking like Skippy. See how quiet Calico Cat is?"

Mrs. Adams nodded, and a pleasant smile softened her sharp features. "It's a precious little kitten. I had a calico cat once, years ago, when I was a little girl." She

73

held out her arms. " May I hold it? "

Tony gulped at the unexpected request, but hastily recovered his wits and shot to his feet. " Yes, indeed! " His eyes shone as he placed the kitten in her outstretched arms.

Mrs. Adams stroked the kitten with a dreamy, faraway look on her smiling face. Cherry held her breath, wondering what Tony would say next.

But before he could continue his persuasive speech, Mrs. Adams surprised them all by saying: " You and Cherry have other kittens, don't you, Tony? Why not let me keep this one? I'd give it a good home — I promise."

Tony's face broke into a glow. " We were thinking about offering her to Bentley for the pet show — "

" Oh, I'd let Bentley enter the little darling in your pet show," Mrs. Adams assured them. " All fixed up with a big ribbon bow."

" Well, then — it's all settled." Tony stepped back with lowered eyes. He dared not look at Cherry for fear they'd both break into a rash of giggles.

Mrs. Adams stood up, holding Calico Cat tenderly in her arms. " I have a little basket that would make a wonderful bed for this baby, and I know just where I can lay my hands on it. Please excuse me — I'm so grateful to you." And she glided happily out of the room.

Bentley stood up, his cheeks flushed a faint pink. " Gee, thanks! Thanks a million. I never dreamed we'd have a pet in this house."

" That's all right, Bentley," Tony murmured. " I'd rather you'd have Calico Cat than anybody else in the world."

74

Cherry swallowed the lump in her throat as she followed Tony toward the door. Their suppressed giggles had softened to warm smiles at the joy of giving a welcome gift.

Bentley walked ahead of them and pushed open the screen door, then drew it back with a sudden stealthy movement. "Wait," he whispered harshly. "Look across the street!"

Cherry and Tony followed his gaze and saw the tall figure of a strange man walking down the curved driveway of the house on the hill. It was no one they had ever seen before, and they watched curiously as he came nearer the street. The stranger wore no hat and his dark-red hair glinted in the sunlight as he turned his head slowly from side to side with jerky nervous glances. Once he looked back quickly over his shoulder.

They could not see the man's eyes in his long, lean face because he was wearing dark sunglasses. He stopped at the foot of the driveway and stared intently up the street and down the street, as if undecided which way to go. Then, shrugging his shoulders, he hurried off with long strides in the direction of Main Street.

"Do you think we should follow him?" Tony burst out.

"No, I don't." Bentley's voice was quiet but firm. "I think we should call the police."

Before they could say any more, Mrs. Adams pattered into the hall behind them. "Come to the kitchen for a minute, please," she called out cheerfully. "Calico Cat is curled up in her basket, perfectly at home."

With fast-beating hearts, they turned and followed her.

For THE MOMENT
Tony, Cherry, and Bentley had each forgotten about
the kitten. Their main concern now was the tall, red-
haired stranger. Who was he and what was he doing on
Captain Gabe's property? Where had he gone in such a
hurry?

Although there was no time to lose, they stood po-
litely in the spotless kitchen and gazed down at Calico
Cat purring contentedly in the dainty basket. Tony felt
sure that he had found a good home for their favorite,
but he squirmed uneasily, wondering if the police
would be able to find the man. He was certainly getting
a good start on them.

Mrs. Adams did not seem to notice the excitement
running like an electric current through the three fig-
ures standing silently around the basket. Her brown
eyes sparkled behind her shining nose glasses. " It was
thoughtful of you to bring us a kitten," she said warmly.

" Bentley and I shall enjoy having Calico Cat for a pet and we want you to come over to see her any time you feel like it."

" Thank you, Mrs. Adams," Tony said, hardly hearing her gracious words. " Thanks a lot. But right now I think we'd better hike for home. Mom will be coming in soon and she won't know where we are."

He paused at the door and looked back at Bentley. " Want to come with us? "

Cherry was surprised to hear Bentley's quick acceptance. For some reason he wasn't acting like a stick-in-the-mud as they eagerly took the short cut through the adjoining back yards.

She noticed two bright spots of color in the pale skin over his thin cheekbones. He seemed to have changed his critical, withdrawn attitude. For the first time, he was really with them instead of against them.

Tony called out a loud " Hello " as they went in the back door, but there was no answer. His mother evidently hadn't returned from her meeting. The house was empty except for Skipper, who waked from a nap and began barking a wild welcome, leaping at Tony's knees as he sat down at the telephone table in the hall.

" I'll call Dad first," he told Cherry and Bentley, who hovered near. " Quiet, Skipper," he commanded, dialing the office number. " I can't hear myself think."

Miss Henshaw's familiar voice answered, " Shipping Department."

" Is Dad there? "

" No, Tony." Miss Henshaw recognized his voice. " He's out in the plant. Want me to have him call you back when he comes in? "

"Oh, golly," Tony mumured in a voice heavy with disappointment.

Miss Henshaw sensed the urgency of the call. "Hold on! Hold on a second. Here he comes!"

Tony's spirits lifted at the sound of his dad's deep, quizzical, "Hello?" and he quickly gave a report of the red-haired stranger, ending grimly, "Don't you think it's a job for the police?"

"I'll call headquarters immediately," his dad said without hesitation. "You wait for us right there at home. We'll pick you up in a jiffy."

Tony replaced the receiver and turned around with a sigh of relief. "Dad's bringing the police," he announced. "We're to wait here for them to pick us up."

"Oh, gr-r-reat!" Cherry gurgled. "We get to ride in the police car!"

"I'd like to go along." Bentley's words were a request rather than a statement.

"Sure," Tony replied. "We'll need you."

Cherry walked to the front door. "Too bad Lynn isn't here to go with us." She brushed the hair back from her forehead with a restless gesture. "I hope they hurry."

"Let's wait on the porch," Tony suggested. "They'll soon be roaring up out front."

Tony and Bentley sat down side by side on the steps, while Cherry danced up and down the walk to the street. She just couldn't sit still. Occasionally she shaded her eyes with one hand and peered excitedly into the slanting rays of the sun. Why didn't they hurry? The minutes seemed like hours.

"Here comes Mom," she squealed suddenly, and

raced forward to give her the news.

As Tony bounded from the steps to join them, he heard Cherry call out, " Oh, Mom, you should have been here! "

" I'm sorry I'm late," Mrs. Parker said, smoothing Cherry's rumpled hair. " The meeting lasted longer than I expected." She smiled from one excited face to the other. " Has something terrible happened? "

Cherry and Tony both burst into a torrent of talking at the same time. Each one was trying to explain that a squirrel had gone in through an open basement window in Captain Gabe's house, and they had followed him in but couldn't find him; that they had later seen a red-haired stranger leaving the premises.

When Cherry stopped for breath, Tony added in a calmer voice: " But don't worry, Mom. Dad is on his way home, and the police are coming too."

Before she could ask any questions, Mr. Parker's car pulled into the driveway and stopped. Then Tony let out a whoop as the black squad car came into view. It looked very important driving up to the curbing. Big white letters stood out on the side, HILLSPORT PO–LICE DEPARTMENT, and the red dome light was flashing on top. The children drew near it in a moment and stood waiting while Mr. Parker stopped for a word with his wife.

" The children called me about seeing a red-haired stranger leaving the hill," he explained. " I phoned headquarters immediately and passed on the description Tony gave me. Detectives were assigned to this area in unmarked cars to scout the neighborhood, and a dispatch was radioed to all police cars to be on the alert. They're combing the town."

" But the man may have been a perfectly innocent person! "

" I hope so. Nevertheless, it's best to find out. We're going up to see if there's any evidence of disturbance at the house. Want to go along? "

Mrs. Parker waved him on with a smile. " I don't think it's necessary. I'll wait here for a report."

Tony was in the height of glory when he was delegated to ride in the front seat to give directions. He sat up very straight between broad-shouldered Sergeant Thomas, whose heavy dark eyebrows almost met over the bridge of his nose, and young Officer Edwards, looking handsome in his blue uniform.

From the rear seat Bentley, Cherry, and Mr. Parker waved good-by to Mrs. Parker as she stood on the porch and watched them drive away.

" Suppose you tell Sergeant Thomas all you know about what's happened while we're on the way," Dad suggested, leaning forward to tap Tony on the shoulder.

Although it was a short distance from their home to the top of the hill, Tony had time to tell most of the day's disturbing events, with frequent promptings from Cherry and Bentley. He was describing the appearance of the stranger when they rolled up the winding driveway and stopped in front of the white-columned porch.

" He was a rather tall man," Tony ended, " and he had red hair."

Young Officer Edwards opened the door and unfolded his six-foot figure out of the car. " I'm sure glad I haven't got red hair," he grinned, then swept off his cap and a mop of curly red hair shone out in the late-

80

afternoon sunshine.

Without thinking, Cherry blurted out impulsively, " Oh, but you have so got red hair! " When she heard the laughter around her, she joined in sheepishly, wishing that she'd caught the joke in time to hold her tongue.

Sergeant Thomas came around the car chuckling good-humoredly and waited until everyone had got out, then his dark eyebrows lowered thoughtfully. " All right, now," he began in a voice that ruled out all further joking, " will you kindly show us which window you found open? "

Tony led the way, and the group followed him around to the west side of the red-brick house and stopped beside the thick bushes. He parted the leaves, and his eyes widened in surprise as he pointed downward. " Th-this one," he stammered. " But it's closed now."

Sergeant Thomas darted a searching look at the window, then at each of the startled faces around him. " Did any of you kids close it? "

" No, sir," Cherry replied meekly.

" No, *sir!* " Tony echoed.

Bentley shook his head vigorously when the piercing eyes fell on him.

" Wait just a minute," Dad said, reaching into his pocket. " I have a key to the front door. I put it on my key ring last night."

" We'll search the house, then, for clues," Sergeant Thomas said, turning abruptly with a determined set to his broad shoulders. " We'll track this thing down."

" Oh, boy! " Tony exclaimed. " I always wanted to

be a detective."

As they retraced their steps, Officer Edwards lifted the cap he was still carrying in his hand and placed it firmly on Tony's head. " How about joining the force? " he suggested with a twinkle in his eye. " We could use a young fellow like you."

The cap was a trifle too big and it slipped down on Tony's forehead, resting heavily on his ears, but he was beaming proudly when they walked inside.

" Maybe we'll find the squirrel with all this good help," Cherry said hopefully.

" That squirrel is probably outside in one of those big trees by now," Sergeant Thomas laughed. " Just hid in here as long as you kids were around."

" Sure, that's right," Cherry said with an emphatic nod. " If I were a squirrel, I would have waited until the coast was clear, then I'd have gone back and jumped right out the window where I came in."

Officer Edwards appeared to be impressed. " Say — you're a pretty good little detective." There was a hint of humor in his voice as he continued, " Would you have closed the window behind you? "

Cherry caught the joke this time and was the first to laugh. " No, I guess not," she admitted, " not if I were a squirrel without any hands."

" We'll find out who did close it," Sergeant Thomas said as he turned and walked from the hall into the long living room.

He stopped for a moment, took in the entire room with a sweeping glance, then walked with heavy strides toward the grand piano. With his hands clasped behind his back, he stared intently at the closed keyboard without saying a word or changing expression. But there was a tenseness in his body that indicated he had discovered something important.

He motioned to the younger man. " Look at that dust," he said as Officer Edwards stepped forward.

Cherry felt her cheeks grow warm with embarrassment. Did he mean they weren't doing a good job looking after Captain Gabe's house? Dad had said last night it was almost time for them to give the place a good airing. She determined to give it a good dusting too.

" I'll bring a dustcloth next time we come up," she apologized.

" Never mind, Miss. I'm glad the dust was here; otherwise I couldn't have seen these fingerprints."

When Sergeant Thomas pointed them out, they could all see prints in the dust along the cover of the keyboard — prints that might have gone unnoticed by a less keen observer.

" Gee! " Tony exclaimed. " Will you have to take the piano to headquarters for examination? "

There was a deep rumble of laughter from Sergeant Thomas. " Well, fortunately — no. That won't be necessary." His laughter was followed by a stern seriousness. " I'll have to get in touch with the Identification Bureau," he explained, " and have them send out a fingerprint expert. He'll bring his kit and a camera right out here where he can make a photograph to take back to headquarters."

" The phone here is disconnected, of course," Mr. Parker said. " Do you want me to go back home and call from there? "

Sergeant Thomas nodded in agreement. " Fine. I'll

84

go with you. Edwards can stay here with the kids in case the red-haired stranger turns up again."

Bentley, who had been watching and listening in absorbed silence, touched the big man's arm in a bold impulse. " Do you think we could go upstairs and look in the study where I saw the light last night? "

" Every room will be searched in due time," Sergeant Thomas assured him, starting for the door into the hall. His footsteps were halted by a tumultuous jangle of bells that seemed to come from all parts of the house.

The sound rolled through their ears in a clashing medley of big bells and little bells, all reverberating together.

CHAPTER

8

T HE DIN OF THE
bells continued without any letup as the two officers
sprang into action, each one reaching for his holster.
They dashed into the hall, followed by Mr. Parker,
leaving Tony, Cherry, and Bentley staring at each other
openmouthed. A glimmer of suspicion entered their
minds at the same instant.

" The squirrel! " Tony snapped his fingers and broke
into a run. The big cap slipped over his eyes, but he
pushed it back, stumbling headlong in his haste to
reach the bells.

" Of course it is." Cherry grabbed Bentley's hand as
he held back and almost dragged him along with her,
talking as she ran. " It's bound to be the squirrel. He
must have jumped into the network of pulleys in the
back hall and set all the bells in the house to ringing.
Surely we'll catch him now," she ended breathlessly,
coming to a halt beside Tony.

She could see a small cocoa-brown animal above the

heads of the men as they stood gaping incredulously at the bell ropes. But the creature causing the commotion certainly wasn't a squirrel.

"Jumping Jehoshaphat!" Sergeant Thomas exploded in laughter. "A blooming monkey! A blooming ring-tailed monkey doing tricks like a circus actor."

"It's somebody's pet that's gotten loose," Officer Edwards said softly. "See there — he's wearing a collar and chain."

He reached for the dangling chain that twitched crazily with the racing antics of the small monkey. "Come on, fellow," he coaxed. "Don't be afraid. You're among friends."

The three children were thoroughly enjoying the spectacle as they watched the monkey slow down and study Officer Edwards with bright beady eyes. He seemed to be considering the man's soothing words.

"Does anybody in the neighborhood own a pet monkey?" Sergeant Thomas inquired, keeping his eyes on the overhead performance.

"Not to my knowledge," Mr. Parker replied, scratching the back of his head. "And I'm sure the children haven't heard of one or we'd know about it."

"This animal is certainly an important clue in the case," Sergeant Thomas went on, his brow furrowed in thought. "If none of you have seen the monkey around here before, he could very well belong to the redheaded stranger who was seen leaving the premises." He took out a handkerchief and wiped his forehead. "The question now before us is, Who was the man? Too bad this little fellow can't talk."

The monkey was hanging by his tail upside down,

but at the sergeant's words he jerked upright and began a rapid-fire chattering that sent the children into peals of laughter.

"He's trying to prove to us that he *can* talk, and he's going to stop clowning and tell us all about it." Officer Edwards grinned and his hand caught the end of the swaying chain. "Trouble is, we can't understand his language."

He gave a gentle tug, and the monkey sprang lightly to his shoulder and began picking through the officer's curly red hair with tiny, humanlike hands.

"We'll have to take him with us till we find the owner. He's evidence, you know." Sergeant Thomas looked questioningly at Mr. Parker. "Can you folks keep him for a while? I'd hate to lock him up in jail."

"Oh, boy!" Tony took off the big cap and waved it enthusiastically. "Could we, Dad? Could we please? He'd be wonderful in our pet show."

Tony was secretly hoping the owner would not be found immediately. What fun it would be to have a monkey in the house to play with — much more exciting than kittens!

Dad hesitated. "Well — we have a house full of pets now — "

"But, Dad," Cherry put in, her eyes pleading, "we gave Calico Cat to Bentley this afternoon, and Mrs. Jackson will soon be coming to take the other two kittens to the farm."

"What about Skipper? Will a dog and a monkey get along together?"

"We'll teach them to be friends," Tony said eagerly. "Please let us give it a try."

Smiling dubiously, their father turned to Sergeant Thomas. "I'll speak to my wife about it when we put in the call to headquarters. Are you ready to go?"

Tony and Cherry smiled at each other confidently. It was as good as settled. Knowing their mother's love for animals, they both felt certain there would be a new pet in the Parker household — at least for a while.

"All right, let's go." Sergeant Thomas marched toward the front door, talking as he moved along. " The rest of you stay here in case anyone turns up. You can wait on the porch with the animal."

Well satisfied with the arrangements, the children trooped through the hall after Officer Edwards. As the car rolled away, the four of them sat down happily on the front steps, the monkey still perched on Officer Edwards' shoulder.

" Let's call him Co-Co," Cherry suggested, hugging her knees in delight. " He's such a pretty brown color."

" Wonder if he could do any tricks for the pet show? " Tony mused, patting the furry head. " How about it? Could you, Co-Co? "

" I think you can count on him being full of tricks." Officer Edwards smiled. " I knew a family once that had a pet monkey, and he'd perform like a clown, standing on his front feet and turning handsprings. The kids used to dress him up in doll clothes, and he loved the attention. You'll find he's a regular show-off."

Tony kept patting the soft, round head, while a thoughtful expression puckered his face. " I don't know what monkeys eat. Maybe you could tell us."

" Sure — milk, bananas, grapes, and vegetables. They're vegetarians. Give him a piece of celery and watch him go for it. There's an old saying that if you feed them meat they'll chew a hole in their tails. Don't know if it's true or not, but that's what I've heard."

" Then we won't try it." Tony pushed the cap up from his forehead as he considered this information. Immediately, Co-Co grabbed at the hand that had been withdrawn and placed it back on his head, greedy for more patting.

" Oh, you like that, huh? " Tony grinned.

" Let me pet him," Cherry said, reaching out eagerly.
" He belongs to both of us."

Bentley frowned up from the bottom step. " He
doesn't belong to either one of you, and I wouldn't get
too attached to somebody else's pet, if I were you."

Now what's the matter with him? Cherry wondered.
Is he going to be critical again? It would be more fun if
Lynn were along instead of Bentley. But before she
could give the matter any further thought, they all began to giggle merrily as Co-Co ran from one to the
other, peering affectionately into each face.

Officer Edwards held fast to the end of the chain, but
there was plenty of slack for Co-Co to move about
freely. Full of mischief, he snatched the policeman's cap
from Tony's head and plunked it down over his own
furry top.

Tony promptly snatched it back. " No, you don't! "
he shouted. " That's mine."

" Just don't forget where you got it," Officer Edwards
said, rumpling the boy's hair. Tony would have felt
that he'd been taken down a peg or two if he hadn't
caught the friendly wink.

He placed the big cap back on his head gravely, and
during the brief silence there came a queer scratching
noise from inside the house. It was only a faint sound,
but very distinct.

Officer Edwards was galvanized into action, and they
all raced after him into the hall. The strange sound was
coming from an old-fashioned umbrella stand just inside the front door.

As they came to a halt and stood there motionless, the

scratching curiously stopped like a dripping faucet that had been turned off. All eyes stared blankly at the tall, round receptacle.

Bentley nudged Tony. "There's Cherry's hollow stump," he whispered. "Bet the squirrel is hiding in there."

Tony nodded grimly and crept forward cautiously, after removing the dark-blue cap from his head. He held it in both hands, out in front of his body, as he stole closer little by little.

Cherry held her breath, standing quietly at Officer Edwards' elbow, while Co-Co sat meekly on his shoulder. No one made a move. This was Tony's act and there was no interference.

Coming close to the umbrella stand, he lifted the cap high in the air and brought it down firmly over the opening. "I got him!" he shouted.

They could hear protesting squeaks and frantic scratching going on inside.

Tony looked around for help. "What do I do now?"

Officer Edwards dumped Co-Co into Cherry's arms and rushed to Tony's aid. "Keep the cap on tight," he ordered. "We'll carry the whole thing outside."

Shuffling and grunting, they managed to move the umbrella stand through the front door and out to the lawn, where it was upended. The squirrel shot out and streaked to a nearby tree, hiding himself among the leafy branches in a split second.

Cherry tilted her head back and sighed as he disappeared. "Too bad we couldn't keep him for the pet show."

"Don't you have enough pets to enter?" Bentley

muttered as he followed the others outside.

Unmindful of the edge in his voice, Cherry beamed at Tony. " You were wonderful — simply wonderful."

" Thanks for the cap," Tony grinned, and handed it over to Officer Edwards just as the squad car rolled up and stopped in the driveway.

Sergeant Thomas stuck his head out of the car window with a puzzled expression. " What's going on? " he demanded, as Mr. Parker slammed the door on the other side and ran around the car.

" Tony caught the squirrel," Cherry squealed, running to meet the two mystified men. " He's up in that tree now where he belongs." Her face fell. " But I do wish we could have kept him."

" Now, look here, young lady — " her father cupped her chin in the palm of his hand, " that's where I put my foot down. Your mother agreed to keep the monkey for a while; in fact, she seemed as jubilant as you and Tony. But no squirrel, please. We're not starting a zoo."

" What's wrong with a zoo? " Sergeant Thomas chuckled. " Seems like your family has a way with animals. How'd you catch that rascal, Tony? "

While Tony was relating the details of the incident, another car arrived with the fingerprint technician from the Identification Bureau. A neat-looking man dressed in a dark-brown business suit jumped out briskly and came toward them, carrying a black kit and a long, box-like camera with a leather handle.

Sergeant Thomas introduced him with a wave of his hand. " This is Mr. Marley, folks. While he's getting the prints, we'll search the rest of the house and grounds. Here, Edwards, give me the monkey. I'll put him in the car for safekeeping until we're ready to go."

Tony touched his dad's arm and whispered, " Do you think Mr. Marley would let us watch him get the fingerprints? "

" I imagine so," Dad replied as they all filed into the house. " I'll ask him."

After pointing out the prints on the piano, Sergeant Thomas motioned to Mr. Parker and Officer Edwards to follow him for the remainder of the search. They seemed in such a hurry to leave that Tony tugged at his dad's arm again, just to remind him.

" Oh, yes," he said, turning back with a smile. " Mr. Marley, would it bother you to have an audience? "

" Not at all — not at all." Mr. Marley's voice and smile were equally cordial. He began to explain the job ahead as Mr. Parker went on to catch up with the others. " We don't need to dust with the fingerprint powder. Plenty of dust here already. Now, in the case of latent fingerprints — that is, invisible ones — it's necessary to use a special powder for bringing them out to be photographed. For instance, on an ordinary white teacup, we would dust the surface with black powder. The powder clings to the faint film of oil left by the fingers, bringing out the detail of the prints in sharp, clear contrast to the smooth surface of the cup. Should the suspected surface be of a dark color or of different texture, other powders are used to bring out the prints." He leaned forward for a closer observation. " It so happens that these prints are plainly visible, and they'll be brought out sharply by the camera."

Cherry, Tony, and Bentley watched with fascination as Mr. Marley stooped and took the special fingerprint camera from its case and continued talking. " I'll make a couple of shots to take back to the laboratory. We'll focus the camera directly on the prints — " He stopped talking as the words were put into action.

In the hush, footsteps could be heard overhead, moving from room to room. Bentley wished that he might be two people — one to watch the fingerprint expert and one to search Captain Gabe's study with the officers and Mr. Parker. He was sure something interesting would turn up in that room.

But there was a question about fingerprints he had always wanted to ask an expert, and this seemed like a good opportunity. When the camera was lowered, he screwed up his courage and blurted it out. " Is it true," he began in a shrill voice, " that fingerprints can be changed? "

Mr. Marley shook his head, smiling. " No matter how they may be injured or scarred during life, fingerprints regrow in the same identical patterns, a lifelong positive identification."

Cherry turned her hands palms up and studied the fine-lined whorls on her finger tips with a feeling of awe. To think that everyone in the world was different! Although people seemed very much alike, they were all different at the edges! It seemed like magic.

" Now, one more shot," Mr. Marley was saying, and she lifted her eyes in order not to miss a single thing.

Having made the shot with expert precision, he glanced around the room. " Was there any indication of how the house might have been entered? Any broken glass or open windows? I'd like to check for other prints."

" Sure," Tony said eagerly. " There was an open window into the basement. We'll show you."

Tony, Bentley, and Cherry led the way, and this time the black kit was opened since there were no visible prints on any part of the window or ledge.

As Mr. Marley worked in the areaway, three pairs of eyes followed every movement as he proceeded about his business.

" What we have to do now," he said, " is bring out the latent prints." He looked into the kit and, after a moment of scrutiny, selected a small bottle of powder. " We dust with a prepared fingerprint powder — like this. Then we brush with this feather duster — so."

Again the contents of the kit were probed. Next the exposed prints were lifted on a piece of transparent tape and mounted on heavy celluloid. This process was repeated several times in various spots about the window.

" Good deal," Mr. Marley finally said with satisfaction. " Now I'll take these in to headquarters. Thanks a lot, kids. You've been very helpful."

" I wonder," Tony said as they pushed out through the bushes, " if there might be any prints around the door to the carriage house." Breaking away, he sprinted across the yard, while the others followed at a short distance.

When he reached the door, he leaned over in a sudden impulse and squinted through the keyhole. Almost immediately, he fell back as if touched by fire.

" There was an eye looking back at me! " he burst out when the others reached his side. " Somebody was spying on us! "

CHAPTER

9

THE TWO POLICE–
men and Mr. Parker had walked up unobserved in the
excitement, and their faces filled with astonishment
when they heard Tony's flustered voice.

" There was an eye looking back at me! " he babbled.
" I saw it! I know I saw an eye! "

Sergeant Thomas spoke up in a tone of disbelief.
" You're right sure of that, are you? "

Tony gulped and nodded his head.

" Did you hear anything? "

" No, sir."

" Did you open the door? "

" It's locked — I think."

While the others waited in baffled silence, Sergeant
Thomas strode to the door and tried to open it, but
without success. " Got a key? " he asked, turning to Mr.
Parker. " Might as well look in while we're here."

" No. Sorry, but I have just the one key," Mr. Parker
told him, " the key to the front door."

Sergeant Thomas squatted on his thick legs and stuck his right eye to the keyhole. "Can't see a blooming thing. It's dark as a dungeon in there." Then, turning to Tony, he patted him gently on the shoulder. "Son, I think you're seeing things — seeing things that aren't there."

"Maybe it was his own eye," Bentley volunteered. "Maybe it was a reflection of some kind."

"Maybe so, maybe so." Sergeant Thomas seemed ready to dismiss the whole incident as overexcitement. He was about to walk away when his attention was drawn to a rope hanging near the door. It was almost concealed by the leafy ivy vine that covered the brick sides of the building, but the sergeant's sharp eyes didn't miss a thing. "What's this rope for?" he demanded.

"It rings the bell on top of the carriage house," Cherry piped up, then waited for Tony to give the details. That bell was his pet subject, but he remained stubbornly silent, his head lowered toward the ground, so Cherry went on. "It's an enormous bell and was once on top of Captain Gabe's boat. After he brought it here, he used to ring it for George to come home, because it could be heard a long way off."

Sergeant Thomas stroked his chin. "Wonder if it could be heard as far away as headquarters." His big hand reached for the rope and gave it a mighty tug. The quiet air was suddenly filled with shattering sound.

As the full, resonant tones reverberated, Sergeant Thomas blinked his eyes. "Blast me! That bell could be heard in the next county."

When the resounding echoes had faded, he went on: "It might be a good idea to give that rope a good hearty haul if you see anything unusual going on up here. We could be on our way in less time than it would take to reach us by telephone."

It was agreed to ring the carriage house bell for an emergency signal, and the group moved slowly back to the cars that were parked in the driveway.

" I hope Co-Co didn't get lonesome waiting for us," Cherry commented.

Any doubt she may have had of the little monkey's ability to entertain himself vanished when the car door was opened. Co-Co had found a package of cigarettes that Sergeant Thomas had left on the front seat, and had busied himself taking them all out and snapping each one in two.

" Golly, what a mess! " Mr. Parker exploded, running his hand through his hair. " Mother said we'd give him a try, but she isn't going to be very happy if our guest turns out to be destructive."

" Don't worry, Dad," Tony assured him as he brushed up every crumb of loose tobacco. " We'll watch him carefully and keep him out of mischief. Won't we, Cherry? "

" I'm glad he wasn't in my car." Mr. Marley's eyes twinkled. It was very seldom that anybody played a trick on the sergeant. But he seemed to enjoy the good-natured kidding, and waved jovially as Mr. Marley told each of them good-by and drove away to finish his work with the fingerprints.

After a last look at the outside of the house, they left the hill. Bentley was silent on the ride down the driveway and thanked the officers for the lift when he got out at his own corner.

While Sergeant Thomas and Mr. Parker talked in the front seat, Officer Edwards gave Tony and Cherry some good advice about caring for Co-Co.

" I don't think he'll be any trouble," he told them, scratching Co-Co under the chin. " He's just playful and no more destructive than a dog or a cat. You can give him the run of the house and he'll get to be like one of the family." He paused as Co-Co reached for his finger. " The folks I knew had a wire cage for sleeping quarters — about four feet square, with newspapers under the wire bottom. He'll curl right up on the wire floor and sleep like a baby. But since you don't know how long you'll have this monkey, you could just fasten his chain to something in the basement and let him sleep there temporarily."

Tony listened to every word, and the minute they had thanked the officers and gone into the house he was ready to start building a cage for Co-Co.

" Let's wait awhile," Mother suggested. " We don't know how soon we'll find the owner." She smiled down at Co-Co perched on her lap. " Cute little fellow, isn't he? "

Cherry, standing beside her chair, reached over and stroked the soft fur. " I wish Lynn could see him. If she hadn't gone on that picnic today, she could have been with us."

" Another day's coming. She can see him tomorrow." Mother handed the monkey to Tony. " You take care of him while Cherry and I get the food on the table. I hear Dad lifting the lids and sniffing at every pan on the stove. He must be starved."

" So'm I." Tony slumped in the chair cushions while

Co-Co ran inquisitive fingers through his hair.

" Of course you are." Mother's voice was gentle and sympathetic. " I know you're all hungry and worn out. We'll eat and get to bed early so you'll feel fresh and rested when we go up tomorrow to open the house for an airing."

" Why couldn't we take a picnic lunch with us? " Tony mumbled, tagging along to the kitchen.

" We could." Mother opened a drawer for the potato masher. " And that's what we'll do if you want to. We can eat in the yard while the house is airing."

Dad moved away from the stove as Mother lifted the lid on a steaming pan of potatoes. " Come on, Tony," he said. " It's a good time for us to introduce Co-Co to Skipper and the kittens. We can also fix a place for him to sleep in the cellar."

Cherry counted out knives, forks, and spoons, preparing to set the table. " Could we ask Lynn and Bentley to go with us tomorrow, Mom? "

" The more the merrier," Mrs. Parker agreed. " Let's ask their mothers too, and have a real picnic."

" Oh, thanks, Mom." With the silverware grasped in her hands, Cherry's arms encircled her mother's waist for a grateful hug. " You're a peach! A picnic sounds like pecks of fun."

Later, when they were all gathered around the table, Mother waited patiently until the dessert was served and everyone seemed relaxed and comfortable.

" I don't want to be inquisitive," she began, " but things have been happening so fast that I can't keep up with the latest developments. Will somebody please fill in the gaps between the time you left here in the police

102

car until you returned weary and wan with a monkey in tow? "

" You like Co-Co, don't you, Mom? " Cherry's voice sounded a bit anxious. " We can keep him, can't we? "

" Of course, honey," Mother reassured her. " For a while, at least — till we find the owner. But I'd like to know if you found the red-haired stranger, and what about the squirrel? I'm completely in the dark."

" Oh, Tony caught the squirrel." Cherry's face shone proudly. " He trapped him in the umbrella stand and carried it out to the yard."

" There wasn't anything to it," Tony said modestly. " Officer Edwards helped me. Now we don't have to worry about the squirrel any more." His face clouded. " We didn't find the red-haired stranger, though."

" But we found fingerprints in the dust on the piano." Cherry wagged her head seriously. " You never saw so much dust."

" It's a good thing the dust was there," Tony put in. " Mr. Marley, the technician, explained everything to us and let us watch him photograph the prints to take to headquarters. He really knows his business."

" Fingerprints? " Mother looked perturbed and turned questioning eyes to Dad, who was finishing his last bite of apple pie with gusto. " Is that why the officer made a phone call while you were talking to me about keeping the monkey? "

" Nothing at all to worry about." He smiled with complete unconcern. Dad's reaction might have been expected. He seemed ready to laugh the whole thing off. " Just circumstantial evidence," he continued, " and overworked imagination."

Cherry was indignant. " You mean there weren't any prints, nor any stranger walking down the drive this afternoon? "

" Nor — nor any eye at the keyhole? " Tony sounded flustered.

Dad reached around the table and put an arm around each of them and gave them a good tight squeeze. " I don't doubt your word for a minute, and neither does Sergeant Thomas. In his opinion, however, there is no great cause for alarm." Dad leaned back and folded his arms with a twinkle in his eye. " They'll go on with their investigation, of course. But has it occurred to you that those fingerprints might easily have been left by one of the search party last night or by one of you children this morning? "

It suddenly flashed through Tony's mind that he had tried to open the keyboard and his eager hands had found it locked. Even the prints that were taken around the window might be their own. Still, there were many questions left unanswered, and he had a few private opinions of his own.

Dad went on talking. " You mustn't worry about it. If there were any danger, I wouldn't want you to go back tomorrow."

After that the discussion turned to plans for the picnic. Bentley and Lynn must be phoned and given an invitation. The rest of the evening Tony and Cherry spent working out details with their mother for the big day ahead, while Dad read the evening paper and took a cat nap in his big easy chair.

The next morning Dad left the key to Captain Gabe's front door hanging on a nail driven in the bulletin

104

board. " Now, what are your plans for the day? " he asked when he was ready to leave for the office.

" We're going up to the hill later for our regular ' open house day,' " Mother told him. " We'll let in some good fresh air."

" And give the house a good dusting too," Cherry added.

" And have a picnic," Tony chortled.

Dad sniffed at the sandwich Cherry was making. " Bologna! My favorite fruit! Wish I could stay home and go with you."

" Better come along," Mother laughed. " There's going to be quite a crowd."

"Lynn and her mother and Bentley," Cherry enumerated. "Mrs. Adams was invited, but she has to stay home to do some cleaning. And Skipper and Co-Co and us."

Dad pretended to be downcast. "Then I'll have to turn down your invitation, because I'm sure there wouldn't be enough bologna sandwiches for me. But I'm glad you have a good crowd going along." He waved from the doorway. "Take care of things, Tony, and everybody have fun."

When the party trudged up the hill a few hours later, everyone was in high spirits. Skippy pranced ahead, disdaining to notice Co-Co, held on his chain by Cherry. Although the little monkey had been trying to make friends with him since the moment they met, Skippy kept a haughty distance.

Tony and Bentley pulled the red wagon holding bottles of soft drinks buried in ice. Mrs. Parker carried a picnic basket, and Lynn helped her mother with a large brown wicker hamper. Cherry had her hands full taking care of Co-Co.

When they rounded the big house to put their picnic baskets on one of the stone benches in the garden, they caught sight of a squirrel drinking from a birdbath, his long tail twitching nervously. He jumped down quickly at their approach as if he were embarrassed to be seen drinking at the birds' watering station, and scampered to a nearby tree.

"Wonder if that's our old friend?" Tony chuckled as he and Bentley halted the wagon. "If he wants to stay friends, he'd better keep outdoors."

As they moved on, Bentley pushed aside the bushes

106

along the house. " That basement window is closed, so he can't get in there again."

Mrs. Parker put her basket down on the stone bench under a shady maple tree and reached into the pocket of her blue denim skirt. " This is the only way to get in," she smiled, holding up the key. " Let's open up. I want to see if Mr. Squirrel has done any damage. By the time we've looked through the house and dusted a bit, we'll be ready for the picnic. Bring Skipper and Co-Co along too."

" I just can't wait for you to see all the gorgeous things in this house, Mimi," Lynn said, taking her mother's arm as they all walked toward the front door. " You'll simply drool when you see the crystal chandelier in the living room and the carved desk in Captain Gabe's study."

Mrs. Wilson puckered her lips in a comical grimace. " I drool easy, don't I, honey? " She squeezed the warm little hand on her arm. " It's mighty nice to get to see the lovely things you've told me about, but remember, we all came up here to do a little work too."

" The ladies can do the work," Tony said, nudging Bentley, as his mother turned the key and pushed open the heavy door. " We'll just supervise and see that it's done right."

" No work, no food." Cherry flicked a dustcloth out of the pocket of her blue jeans and tossed it at her brother. " You were so anxious to dust off the stair railing before, now you can do it right."

" Oh, no," Tony grinned. " That's squaw work." He dodged expertly and the dustcloth landed on the carpet.

Bentley leaned over and picked it up. " I don't mind

dusting," he said amiably. " I'm used to it, helping my mother with the dusting and cleaning. I could run the vacuum cleaner if you want me to."

" No electricity — remember? " Tony said with obvious satisfaction. " And get rid of that dustcloth. We men aren't going to do women's work."

" Don't worry, young man," his mother said placidly as she took the cloth and gave it back to Cherry. " There's a job for everyone. You and Bentley can unlock the windows and open them. That ought to be heavy enough work to suit your manly pride."

" Sure — fine. That's what we'll do." Tony grabbed Bentley's arm and headed for the living room.

Mrs. Parker took another dustcloth from her own pocket and shook out the folds. " Cherry, you and I can get busy on the dusting while Lynn shows her mother around."

" But I want to help," Mrs. Wilson protested. " I can see everything as we go along. I'm an old hand at dusting, just like Bentley. Why not let the girls take care of Co-Co and Skipper while we dust? "

" We'll make good nursesmaids for a dog and a monkey," Lynn giggled. " Which one do you want for your baby, Cherry? "

At that moment, Tony and Bentley whizzed through the hall on their way to the dining room. Bentley overheard Lynn's question and shouted back at her, " You take the monkey — it looks like you."

Lynn turned to her mother, frowning, as the boys disappeared with muffled giggles. " Did you hear that, Mimi? I always have trouble with him."

" Never mind, honey. He was only teasing you,"

108

Mrs. Wilson drawled. " If you'd had as many brothers as I had, you'd be used to that. Think nothing of it."

" I'll take care of Co-Co," Cherry offered hastily. She wrapped the chain around her wrist and placed him on her shoulder. " Skipper will take care of himself. All you have to do is keep an eye on him."

They followed Mrs. Parker into the living room. " This won't be too big a job," she said, looking around with an appraising eye. " The main thing I'm concerned about is to see if everything is in good condition after the squirrel's visit."

With Cherry's help, she began to lift the white sheets covering the big easy chairs and the couch. Then she scrutinized the carpet in every corner to see if any holes had been chewed. When she was ready to start dusting, Mrs. Wilson joined her, having admired and praised all the objects of beauty Lynn pointed out to her.

They proceeded methodically from room to room. The curtains at the open windows stirred softly in a slight breeze, showing the progress of the boys in carrying out their job. Later, they all met in Captain Gabe's study where Bentley and Tony were holding a low conversation in front of the desk. The boat model once more held their rapt attention.

Mrs. Parker sank into the depths of the red leather chair, satisfied that no damage or disturbance was evident in any part of the big house. She smiled at the bubbling enthusiasm of the children showing Mrs. Wilson the pictures on the walls and all the details of the desk and the *Edna M.*

Finally she glanced at her wrist watch. " As soon as you can tear yourselves away and give Mrs. Wilson a rest, I think we ought to spread out the picnic. It's already past noon and if you're as hungry as I am, a little nourishment will be welcome."

" What's become of Skipper? " Lynn whirled around, suddenly remembering her job. " I thought he came in with us." Her eyes darted around the room. " Wasn't he here just a minute ago? "

" No," Mrs. Parker said, rising from her chair. " I don't believe I've seen him in this room at all."

" Maybe he was hungry and went to get the lunch ready," Cherry suggested playfully as she followed her mother into the hall.

As the others came out looking from side to side, the sound of Skipper's blustering bark broke out in the hall below. They all rushed pell-mell down the stairs in time to see the bristling dog shoot out the open front door, yapping furiously.

10

Tony WAS THE first one to reach the door and see the rattling old truck coming up the driveway. When it jerked to a halt in the loose gravel, he paused on the steps to look closer, then turned around with a broad grin on his face.

" No cause for alarm," he called back, imitating his father's casualness. " It's just Mrs. Jackson and Harmon."

He raced out to greet them, followed quickly by his mother and Cherry, whose anxious expressions had changed to smiles of welcome. Mrs. Wilson and Lynn waited on the porch with Bentley as the stout, gray-haired woman dressed in a neat black-and-white print dress got out of the truck cab. She straightened her black straw hat with a red rose bobbing on the brim, then shook a plump finger at the excited dog.

" What's all the hubbub about, Skipper? " she asked with affectionate severity. " Don't you know us any more? "

Skipper's menacing tone changed to friendly yipping the minute he recognized Captain Gabe's housekeeper of many years. His feathered tail fluttered joyfully as he joined his welcome to that of the Parkers.

"He's forgotten the many times I fed him and cleaned up after him when he was a puppy," Mrs. Jackson joked. She put her arms around Tony and Cherry. "But I guess you take mighty good care of him now, and a dog is always fondest of the one who is feeding him."

"Oh, I think he's still fond of you," Tony said tactfully. "He just wants everybody to know he's guarding this property."

"And that's good — that's a good dog." Mrs. Jackson nodded her head approvingly. Then she turned and called out sharply to her son, who was sitting stolidly behind the steering wheel, staring straight ahead. "Harmon! Harmon, aren't you going to get out? Come looka here what Cherry's got riding on her shoulder!"

When the large, rawboned figure climbed out and lumbered toward them, Mrs. Parker said graciously, "We were just getting ready to eat a picnic lunch and I do hope you'll stay and eat with us." She turned toward the porch. "I want you to meet our friends, the Wilsons, and I think you remember Bentley."

After the introductions were acknowledged, Lynn wondered how such a surly-looking man could have such a nice cozy mother as Mrs. Jackson. His coarse-featured face didn't even crack a smile when his eyes came to rest on Co-Co.

But Cherry seemed not to mind his looks. She

112

blithely handed the monkey over to him, saying: " This is Co-Co. We'll tell you all about him while we're having lunch."

" Thank you for the invitation," Mrs. Jackson smiled, " but farm folks don't keep the same hours as you do. We had our breakfast so early that we were hungry as wolves about eleven thirty. So we finished our errands and had a hamburger in town. Harmon dearly loves hamburgers."

" Well, I'm glad you stopped to see us anyway," Mrs. Parker said heartily.

" I wanted to see you before we started for home," Mrs. Jackson went on, " and I wanted to find out if the kittens were ready to take back to the farm. When we didn't locate you at home, I decided you might be up here."

Cherry's face lighted up. " The kittens are ready — we've given one to Bentley. I'll run right home and get them for you."

When she made a move to leave, Mrs. Jackson held her arm. " No hurry — no hurry at all. We can get them next time we're in town. I don't want to hold up your picnic."

" It will take a few minutes to get ready," Mrs. Parker said, " and Cherry can be back by then. We can have a visit while she's gone and give you the latest news."

Lynn offered to go along, and the two girls set off in a jog trot down the hill.

On the way back each one carried a kitten curled in her arms and they slowed down to a walk. They hadn't talked much after leaving the hill to save their breath for running, but now Cherry could see that Lynn had something on her mind she was bursting to talk about.

" What's the matter, Lynn? " she asked with a side-long glance. " You look very broody."

Lynn frowned thoughtfully. " I don't like to be suspicious of your friends, but I still think the Jacksons have more to do with that lost will than just being witnesses. Maybe it's none of my business, but you asked me and I'm telling you what I think."

Cherry shifted the kitten to her other arm before she spoke. The kittens were getting heavier every day and hungrier, but they would soon have plenty of milk from Harmon's cow and Mrs. Jackson would give them a good home. How could Lynn think anything bad about the Jacksons?

She shook her head slowly. " You're wrong, Lynn. Mrs. Jackson is a fine woman. Captain Gabe trusted her about everything and treated her like one of his own family."

" Maybe so, but that son of hers — ugh! " Lynn shivered. " I wouldn't trust him. He was probably the one who opened that basement window, and I'll tell you a good reason why I think so."

Cherry hugged the kitten closer and wondered what was coming next.

Lynn's eyes narrowed as her bouncing step slowed dramatically. " Do you remember the hamburger bun we found on the basement table? " She smiled triumphantly. " Mrs. Jackson said her son dearly loved hamburgers. Doesn't that mean anything to you? "

Cherry smiled blandly. " Sure. Everybody likes hamburgers. I dearly love them myself."

114

" You're not a very good detective." Lynn shook her head in despair. " Or maybe you're just hungry. Let's hurry."

The two girls broke into a run for the last lap up the driveway. Cherry really was hungry, and she hoped the picnic baskets had been opened and everything spread out waiting for them. But she had to conceal her disappointment when she saw that they were all still standing around the porch steps just as when she and Lynn had left them.

" My goodness, you made a quick trip." Mrs. Jackson beamed, holding out her arms for the kittens. " Thank you, girls. I was so interested hearing about your adventures, it seems like you're back in no time at all."

Tony jumped from the back of the truck where he and Bentley had sat dangling their feet. " I told them about the leftover hamburger," he told Cherry, " and Harmon says it doesn't sound like imagination to him."

Cherry lowered her eyes as Lynn darted a meaningful glance in her direction. She bit her lip and prayed hard that Lynn wouldn't say anything embarrassing. But whatever her friend might be thinking was discreetly kept silent.

Mrs. Jackson clicked her tongue rapidly. " It doesn't sound good to me at all. I'd sure keep a sharp lookout."

Harmon rose abruptly from the steps where he sat holding Co-Co. " We'd better get going." His voice was gruff, but the flicker of a smile crossed his face as he handed the monkey to Cherry and hurried toward the truck.

With the kittens clasped to her bosom, Mrs. Jackson's

eyes suddenly misted with tears. " It's been a nice visit. Please drive out to see us sometimes — I get a little lonesome, you know." She blinked several times to clear the blur, and the red rose bobbed on her hat as she continued emphatically: " And I do hope that new will turns up soon. I know the Captain would have loved to have you children use the carriage house for your play acting."

When the farewells were over, the truck started away with a noisy scraping of gears. Cherry swallowed the lump in her throat and fell in step with Lynn as the two girls followed their mothers, who were heading briskly for the stone bench under the maple tree. Tony and Bentley lingered on the steps, watching the truck disappear from sight.

Cherry soon recovered her usual cheerfulness in the bustle of opening the baskets and setting out the mouth-watering array of food. Mrs. Wilson had baked a chocolate cake especially for their picnic that brought delighted admiration.

" Just wait till the boys see that! " Cherry stood on tiptoes, dancing up and down with Co-Co bouncing on her shoulder. " It's almost too beautiful to eat."

" They won't get anything to eat if they don't show up soon," her mother said, trying to twist the lid on a jar of olives. " I wish Tony would come and open the olives and pickles. I never did have any strength in my wrists."

" I'll go get him," Cherry offered, and bounded away on flying feet.

When she came around to the front of the house, her footsteps faltered. The boys were nowhere to be

116

seen. While she was wondering where they might have gone, the soft strains of music came faintly from inside the house. Piano music! Someone was playing George's piano — the piano that was locked! Her feet moved slowly forward, as if drawn against her own will, as the chords became louder and more assured.

She crept mouselike up the front steps and through the open door. With trembling knees, she slipped quietly across the hall carpet and stopped wide-eyed in the doorway of the living room.

There stood Tony beside the grand piano watching Bentley's fingers move lovingly over the ivory and black keys. Bentley was playing his recital piece, the one she had heard him practicing many times during the summer. She stood transfixed, unable to move or to speak while the music rose to a crescendo.

It was not until the sound of running feet on the steps outside jarred her back to reality that she could believe her ears or her eyes. The swell of the music must have reached into the garden, for her mother and Lynn and Mrs. Wilson came racing into the hall and stopped breathlessly at her side.

" I thought the piano was locked! " Mrs. Parker cried out. Her voice was incredulous.

" I thought so too," Tony said, looking up as Bentley's hands fell from the keyboard guiltily. " But it wasn't."

" But how did you happen to find out? " his mother questioned him, as he and Bentley came toward them with sheepish smiles.

" Bentley and I got to talking about the fingerprints after the Jacksons left and I decided to come in and see

if I could remember just where my hands touched the cover the day I tried to open it. Dad seemed to think the prints were mine, but I barely touched it the day we found it locked, and Bentley and I agreed that there were more here for Mr. Marley to photograph than I could possibly have left." Tony shrugged his shoulders. " As you see, it isn't locked now."

" No — it isn't locked now," his mother repeated in a puzzled voice. " That's obvious." Then she laughed as if to shake off her bewilderment. " But please close it right away, and let's eat before we have any more interruptions."

It was a welcome suggestion, and they all went outside again, leaving the curtains stirring softly at the open windows.

Cherry unfastened Co-Co's chain and put him on the ground where he could stretch his legs a bit. Then, while she and her mother set out the rest of the food, Mrs. Wilson spread a bright-colored patchwork quilt on the grass. " This is our picnic quilt," she said gaily. " Lynn and I always take it along to sit on when we go picnicking. There's room for all."

Tony, who had finished opening the jars, made a dive for the middle. " Oh, boy, this is solid comfort." He rolled over to find he had company. " Go away, Skipper! She didn't mean you."

With his tail drooping, the crestfallen dog began to walk around the edge of the quilt, eying Tony accusingly.

Co-Co, glad to have his chain removed, sat quietly under the stone bench, bright-eyed and well behaved, watching Skipper intently. Suddenly he darted out and leaped gracefully to the dog's back and balanced himself perfectly in standing position.

Skipper, more surprised than alarmed, broke into a trot, and a delighted audience watched as Co-Co put on an expert performance: now standing, now crouching, now turning a flip — never once losing his poise.

Skipper finally ran to Cherry's side and looked up into her face as if to say, " What's the meaning of all this? " Everyone broke into wild applause.

" A perfect act for the pet show! " Tony shouted.

Cherry broke off a piece of bologna. " Here, Skippy. You deserve a reward." She turned back to the bench. " And here's a piece of celery for Co-Co."

" That's right," her mother said approvingly. " Give encouragement with little treats and I think you can easily train them to give a polished performance for your show."

Like a clap of thunder in a cloudless blue sky, a man's deep voice boomed out: " Bravo! That was indeed an excellent exhibition — worthy of any show I ever saw."

No one had noticed his approach, but every head turned at these startling words, and there he stood — the tall, red-haired stranger, only a few feet from the bright-colored quilt!

11

PLEASE ALLOW ME to introduce myself," the stranger said, and bent to pet Skipper. The dog was sniffing suspiciously at his trouser leg. "My name is Tim Hardesty, of Newark, New Jersey."

Of course this meant nothing to his listeners, but he drew out a card from his wallet and handed it to Mrs. Parker. If he felt uncomfortable under the critical stares, his agreeable smile gave no indication of it.

Mother read the card as he went on talking. " As you see, I am a representative of Field's Investment Company — a traveling representative. I became acquainted with Captain Fellows several months ago at the airport at Louisville while we were waiting for our planes to carry us in opposite directions. We talked at great length. He was a fine old gentleman, very friendly and very eloquent, if I may say so."

That must mean talkative, Tony decided, as he began to warm up to the stranger. If he was a friend of Captain Gabe's, he was a friend of theirs too.

After a brief pause indicating his respect for the old man's memory, Mr. Hardesty continued: " I was hoping to meet his relatives if I should happen to be in this territory. When my business brought me back to the Middle West, I determined to take advantage of this opportunity. I travel by plane, but I took a bus over here from the county seat, since Middleboro is only a few miles away." He smiled down at Skipper, who by this time had accepted him as a friend instead of foe and was jumping up for more petting. " The house was closed when I came by yesterday, and I was afraid that you might be out of town. I didn't want to miss seeing you if it were at all possible, so I came back again today before leaving for my next stop."

" None of Captain Gabe's relatives are here at present," Mrs. Parker hurried to explain. " We are friends and neighbors of the family. This is Mrs. Wilson and I am Mrs. Parker. We came up this morning to air out the house according to agreement with the court." She smiled and waved her hand at the food spread out temptingly on the stone bench. " We are also about to have a picnic, as you see."

" Won't you have a sandwich? " Tony offered eagerly. " D'you like bologna or cheese better? "

The man shook his head with an appreciative grin at Tony. " Thank you very much indeed. I like them both and the food looks wonderful, but I must be on my way as I have to catch the next bus back to Middleboro."

" Oh, I wish you could stay and tell us more about Captain Gabe," Cherry said, holding Co-Co tenderly in her arms.

But you could see that Mr. Hardesty was in a hurry. His face grew serious as he turned to Mrs. Parker. ' Since you are friends of the family, I'd like to pass on to you part of the conversation I had with Captain Fellows that day, in case it is of any importance. As I told you, the Captain and I became acquainted in a short time, and while we were chatting together over our lunch in the airport dining room, he remarked jokingly: ' I bought a big wad of insurance they offered me when I started this trip, and it set me thinking. If anything should happen to me, no one would know where I put my new will. Should have told somebody.' The old man stopped talking then as the waitress served our dessert, but I heard him murmur something about its being safe in the *Edna M.*"

" Why — that's his boat! " Tony exclaimed.

" Yes, I know." Mr. Hardesty said quietly. " He had told me about his boat on the river near here. It seemed like a strange place to put his will, but I didn't question him further, of course. After I learned of the accident, I recalled our conversation and thought this information might be of some help. I hope I'm not too late."

" You're not," Mrs. Parker told him gravely. " And I'm sure it will be appreciated."

" If I can be of any further assistance, you have my name and Field's address on the card. You can reach me through the company I work for at any time."

Having delivered his message, Mr. Hardesty told them all good-by. " Have a nice picnic, good people," he said. " Sorry I can't join you."

" Well! " Cherry burst out as they watched the lanky

figure disappear down the driveway. "That's one mystery cleared up."

"Really two," Bentley corrected her. "The identity of the red-haired stranger is one and the location of the will makes two."

"Can we go search the boat, Mom?" Tony asked eagerly. "Why can't we go right now — soon as we eat?"

"Perhaps we should. I'll phone Dad as soon as we get back home and see what he thinks about it." Mrs. Parker began to pass around the paper plates and napkins. "If anyone is still hungry after all the excitement, just pitch in and help yourself. I've almost lost my appetite."

"Not me!" Tony shouted. "I could eat that whole cake by myself."

"This is a beautiful spot," Mrs. Wilson said when everyone had finally settled down to eating. "If I could get hold of a sickle and lawn mower, I'd like to do a little manicuring on this lawn. I don't get enough outdoor exercise living in a second-floor apartment. Maybe you kids would like to help me, and we'd have another picnic."

"Sure we could." Tony munched his sandwich happily. "We've got plenty of tools at our house."

Lynn gazed toward the carriage house. "Then it would look pretty when the Be Dramatic Club starts giving shows up here."

Cherry sighed. "I hope we find the will. Then we could ask the rightful owners. Do you think we'll find it today, Mom?"

"The boat's a long way up the river, you know,

Cherry. Even if we get permission from the court — "

" I'd be glad to take you," Mrs. Wilson suggested. " My car is always at your service. Our dad's gone again and we're foot-loose and fancy-free."

Mrs. Parker thanked Mrs. Wilson for her offer as she cut the chocolate cake in nice, generous wedges. " If we can make the proper arrangements," she smiled, " we might just as well make a day of it."

" Oh, if we could only find the will! " Lynn burst out. " Wouldn't it be wonderful! "

" Wouldn't it, though? " Bentley's voice dripped with sarcasm. " But I don't think you're going to."

Tony looked at his friend curiously. What made Bentley sound so emphatic? Mr. Hardesty had given them Captain Gabe's exact words. At least, they had accepted his story as true, and there seemed no reason to doubt the man's integrity and honest desire to be helpful. He surely wouldn't have taken all the trouble to come to Hillsport with a cock-and-bull story.

Bentley and Lynn continued to squabble until Mrs. Parker's soft voice came like soothing oil on troubled water. " Well, it must be someplace, and perhaps we can drive up to Bingham's Landing before the day is over and see for ourselves. In the meantime, we'll have to get busy and close the house again just as soon as we finish our cake."

Later as Tony and Bentley went through the house lowering the windows and turning the locks, Tony asked him point-blank, " What made you say we weren't going to find the will? "

" It just doesn't make sense. Captain Gabe was eccentric, sure — but he was too smart to hide a will on that old boat. It was dismantled a long time ago and he'd brought everything he valued back home. You said so yourself."

" Yeah," Tony agreed, then stopped to ponder this reasoning of Bentley's. " But they've looked everywhere in the house without success. And it has to be somewhere." He walked slowly down the stairs, thinking out loud. " Mr. Hardesty was the last one we know who talked with Captain Gabe. I don't see any reason why he couldn't have hidden it in the *Edna M*. He used to go up there often to talk over old times with Mr. Bingham and rummage around the boat."

Bentley seemed absorbed in his own thoughts and said nothing as the two boys walked through the lower hall toward the front door, where Mrs. Parker was waiting with the key in her hand.

Tony threw his arm around Bentley's shoulder. There was no use arguing over something neither one of them was sure about. " Oh, well," he said pleasantly, " we'll have a lot of fun anyway, seeing the boat and all."

By the middle of the afternoon, the Parkers were back home making preparations for the trip. Mother had phoned Dad, and while she was waiting for him to call back, Tony hunted for his flashlight.

" We may need it for searching in dark corners," Tony explained to Cherry, who was helping him look around his room. " Bentley thinks it's a wild-goose chase, but he may be surprised."

" I hope so. He's so high and mighty." Cherry walked to the bed and lifted a pillow. " There's your flashlight, right where you left it. Men can't find anything."

126

" I was excited when I put it there," Tony grinned.
" Thought I might need it in case anyone showed up
in the night."

Cherry wagged her head. " You're getting as full of
imagination as Bentley."

Just then the phone rang, and they both dashed out of the room. They could hardly wait until Mother had finished talking and finally hung up. The news was good. Dad had got in touch with the proper authorities and received permission to search for the will. Another phone call was made to Mrs. Wilson, telling her that everything was all set to leave for the *Edna M.,* tied up in the quiet harbor up the river several miles.

Tony felt too excited to sit still and wait for the car to come for them. " Instead of phoning Bentley, I'll just run over and get him. Be back in a jiffy." He flung the last words over his shoulder as he raced through the kitchen and let the back screen door slam shut in his haste.

" We'll leave Skipper at home. He'll be safer in his own back yard," Mother told Cherry. " He probably wouldn't stay close to the crowd with so many inviting distractions on the riverbank to lure him into mischief."

" Could we take Co-Co? " Cherry asked hopefully. " The little fellow hardly knows us and he might think he was abandoned if we left him at home the very first day."

It was agreed to let the monkey go along when Cherry promised to keep a firm hold on his chain.

As soon as they heard the horn of the Wilsons' car give three lively beeps, Cherry and her mother were on their way to the curbing, where Lynn and Mrs. Wilson sat smiling in the front seat.

" I'll sit in back with the boys," Mrs. Parker said.

Cherry climbed in beside Lynn. " Tony's gone to get Bentley," she explained. " They'll be right back."

128

But the minutes dragged on and the girls began to grow impatient, wondering what could be causing the delay.

" I guess I'll have to go get 'em." Cherry put one foot out of the car door just as Tony showed up.

" Bentley's not coming," he said shortly, stepping into the back seat with his mother. " Said he had things to do."

" Now what's come over that crazy boy? " Lynn muttered. " D'you suppose he has to stay home and tidy the house? "

" He wouldn't tell me," Tony said with a disappointed sigh. " Wouldn't tell me anything. Just acted kind of funny and kept his eyes down all the time I was begging him to come on."

" Don't worry about it," Mrs. Wilson drawled. " You just tell me which way to go and forget about Bentley."

Tony perked up and leaned forward, giving directions, as the party set off in the spirit of high adventure, determined to let nothing dampen the glow of this exciting moment.

CHAPTER

12

M<small>RS. WILSON THEN</small>
guided the car at Tony's directions through the late-
afternoon traffic of Hillsport's water-front street, past
the fish markets and warehouses. Soon they were passing the neat flower-bordered lawns of the homes facing
the river on the outskirts of town.

Tony began to relax a little when they reached the
highway, and leaned back to enjoy the cool rush of air
on his flushed cheeks. Cherry and Lynn were chattering
happily, and he felt a twinge of disappointment that
Bentley wasn't with them for him to talk to. It baffled
him to think that Bentley had refused to come along
without giving any reasonable excuse. But he made up
his mind to quit worrying about it.

After spinning along the highway for several miles
out of town, the car turned into a dirt road and wound
through river-bottom cornfields, with Tony calling the
turns.

" Gee, this bumpy road looks like it leads to the end

of nowhere." Lynn tried to sit up very straight, bouncing first against Cherry and then against her mother. " Not many cars go this way, I bet."

" Not many," Tony laughed. " Just the farmers who live down here and people who keep their boats at Mr. Bingham's dock."

After making several right-angle turns between the rows of tall corn growing on both sides of the road, they finally saw the sign BINGHAM'S LANDING. The river sparkled ahead of them through the trees along the bank.

When Mrs. Wilson stopped the car under the shade of a clump of willows and turned off the motor, they could hear the high, thin whistling of an old familiar hymn.

" That must be Mr. Bingham," Mrs. Parker smiled. " He's always whistling a hymn. ' Jesus Loves Me ' is his favorite, although he sometimes makes up tunes as he goes along."

As they walked toward the wooden dock, the old man arose stiffly from his weather-beaten rocking chair, stopped whistling, and squinted at them through nearsighted blue eyes. His face was tanned and looked like a piece of well-aged leather under a stubble of gray beard. Recognition of the Parkers widened his eyes and a welcoming grin creased his cheeks into gullies.

" Well now, I reckon," he rasped, coming toward them, " you're a sight for sore eyes — that's a fact. Coming to pay the old man a visit or coming to see the Old Lady? "

" He calls the *Edna M.* ' Old Lady,' " Cherry whispered to Lynn.

Mrs. Parker held out her hand. " We want to see you and the boat too. These are our friends, Mrs. Wilson and her daughter, Lynn. They've never seen the *Edna M.* and we'd like to poke around for a while if you don't mind."

" Wal, just help yourselves." He raised his eyebrows as Co-Co jumped from Cherry's arms and teetered toward him. " What kind of a varmint you got there on that chain? "

" It's a ring-tailed monkey," Cherry explained. " His name is Co-Co. We're keeping him for — for somebody."

The old man chuckled. " I'll sit here and mind him for you whilst you're on the boat if you want me to."

Cherry could see that Co-Co and Mr. Bingham had made friends on sight. She was glad to leave him on the dock in good hands to be free for the serious business ahead.

When they crossed from the dock to board the *Edna M.,* Lynn's face glowed with interest. Her eyes roved up and down at the different kinds of boats tied up in the water. There were cabin cruisers, high-powered motorboats, and speedboats; skiffs, rowboats, and small fishing boats. But the most fascinating of all was the *Edna M.,* in spite of her run-down appearance.

It was a much bigger boat than she had expected to see. The white paint was peeling and the interior was stripped bare of all its former grandeur, but the very walls seemed haunted by the glory of bygone years. In her imagination, Lynn could see the *Edna M.* as a floating palace.

For the next half hour, they made a tour of explora-

133

tion. The main deck was bare and desolate. All partitions had been removed and the machinery, including the huge engine, had long since been sold.

" This doesn't look very promising." Mrs. Parker shook her head with a wan smile and turned to Tony. " Well, where do we go from here? "

" Let's start at the bottom and look down the hull," Tony suggested, and ran toward the stairs that went below deck. He stopped at the foot of the creaky steps and turned his flashlight from side to side in the gloomy darkness.

Peering over his shoulder as the others crowded behind her, Lynn shuddered. " Gee, it's spooky down here." Then she let out a sudden squeal when a passing log floated against the boat with a thump. " This is too creepy," she whimpered. " Let's go back up. There's no place down here to hide a will."

" I think you're right," Mrs. Parker agreed, turning to ascend the creaking stairs.

" Interesting, though," Mrs. Wilson observed. " I like to hear the lap of the waves from the outside."

Back on the first deck, sunshine flooded through the many openings, but the bare walls and bare floor offered no possible place to search. The side walls, rising to heavy girders overhead, were barren as a stony cliff.

Each deck was equally disappointing. They were faced with long vistas of emptiness. When they entered the quarters where the crew had slept, there was nothing to be seen but an old mattress on the floor. After turning it over and investigating every seam, Mrs. Parker shook her head. " I doubt very much that he would have put it in there anyway."

They moved on to the middle area, where the crew ate, and Tony let out a whoop when he spied an old icebox in one corner. " Now! There's a good place to hide a will."

" D'you think he wanted to keep it cool? " Cherry giggled, and winked at Lynn as the two girls skipped across the floor.

They all gathered around him and looked over his shoulder while he examined the shelves and peeling walls. " Nuts," Tony frowned. " No luck at all."

" Everything seems to be skinned down pretty well," Mrs. Parker observed. " There's just no logical place to hunt."

" Nothing left but the pilothouse," Cherry said dismally. Then her face brightened. " But you'll like it up there, Lynn. It's the most interesting part of the boat, I think."

They climbed up the steep, narrow steps and stopped to look into the waste room below the pilothouse. The pilot wheel was so large that it extended through the floor into this small space which was used to store ropes and other equipment. Tony pointed out the brake shoes, one on either side of the big wheel, while his mother and Mrs. Wilson peered around looking for a likely place to search.

" We might as well give up," Mrs. Parker said finally, " and enjoy the view from above."

Up another short flight of stairs into the glass-enclosed room, the group was rewarded by the broad vision of the river flowing peacefully below.

Tony slipped behind the wheel into the comfortable seat securely fastened to the floor, where the pilot sat to guide the boat. "You can look out from here," he announced, "and see far and wide in any direction."

"Oh, let me try that seat," Lynn begged eagerly. "May I touch the wheel?"

"Sure," Tony said, readily giving up the place of honor. "Only, you won't be going anywhere. We're tied up to the dock, remember."

It was a thrill, whether they were moving or not, to clasp the smooth wooden knobs in each hand and feel the power that must lie behind the slightest move. After the children took turns behind the handsome pilot wheel, Tony called their attention to the ropes with wooden handles that came up through the floor onto a panel board.

"These are the ropes to pull for the signal bells to ring," Tony told them. "Of course, the bells aren't on the boat any more, but this is where the pilot used to control the course of the boat — from right here."

Lynn began to read aloud from the labels on the panel board. "Slow, Speed Ahead, Astern, Engine Room —" she broke off suddenly. "Like the bells in Captain Gabe's house, only there they mean different things, just like you told us."

"Sure. Same principle," Tony nodded, then turned as his mother touched him on the shoulder.

"I hate to break this up," she said, "but if we're going to stop for a word with Mr. Bingham, we'd better get started. There's simply no place here to look further for the will."

Back on the dock, Mr. Bingham's crinkled smile showed his pleasure in seeing his old friends again. "Come sit down a spell." He waved a gnarled hand in a gesture of hospitality. " Hope you don't mind these hard benches. One of the ladies can take my rocker."

Tony and Cherry were glad to hear their mother accept the invitation as she sat down on one of the wooden benches and motioned to Mrs. Wilson to have a seat in the rocking chair. It was always fun to visit with Mr. Bingham. He was one of their favorite people, and they loved to hear him talk, even when he told the same stories over and over again.

" How about a nice cold drink? " he said when everyone was seated. " The pop case is full. Have to keep it ready for the folks that pull in here to tie up their boats."

" Let's see if I have some nickels," Mrs. Parker said, opening her purse.

Mr. Bingham shook his head vigorously. " No — no! Put that away," he insisted. " The treat is on me. What'll it be? Strawberry, orange, lemon, lime, root beer? Got 'em all."

After taking their orders, Mr. Bingham handed Co-Co over to Cherry and shambled to the pop case under the trees, with Tony at his elbow to help carry the bottles back.

Lynn could hardly wait until everyone settled down so the old man could start talking. Tony had said he was almost as interesting as Captain Gabe himself. They had been friends, and maybe he would tell them something about the Captain, or about making the model of the *Edna M.*

Slowly and deliberately he took out his pipe and lighted it, while the others were quenching their thirst. Finally he spoke. " I sure hate to see the Old Lady go

137

to rack and ruin," he sighed, turning his age-dimmed eyes toward the *Edna M.* " In all the years I spent aboard as carpenter, she was kept in the best shape of any boat that ever kicked up the whiskers all up and down the river."

When Lynn looked puzzled, Tony put in eagerly, " ' Kicking up the whiskers ' means the paddle wheel is churning the water so fast it wears a beard of white foam."

" Do boats have carpenters? " Mrs. Wilson asked curiously.

" Yes, ma'am. 'Deed they do." Mr. Bingham's eyes grew mellow as he began to reminisce. " I had my own little cubbyhole just off the engine room where I kept my tools and workbench. There was never a day I wasn't busy, doing a little painting, making repairs here and yon." He broke off with a little cackle. " But I still found time to make a model of the Old Lady. Made it to scale. Took me nigh onto three years, but I finished it down to the last notch and gave it to Cap'n Gabe for a present."

" I've seen it," Mrs. Wilson said, with admiration in her voice. " I don't see how in the world you did it."

" Wal, I'll tell you." Mr. Bingham drew on his pipe and smiled happily. You could see that he took great pride in his work. " I found me a block of wood for the hull — just a piece of planking — and sawed it to rough shape. Then I planed it down and sanded it smooth. After that I cut out another piece of wood and went to work on the next deck and the next, just like building a house, putting up one story after tother."

"But the detail," Mrs. Wilson marveled. " It's fan-

138

tastic that you could have made all those intricate pieces by hand."

"No other way," Mr. Bingham said proudly. "I whittled all the fancy work — paddle wheel, smokestacks, 'scape pipes, railings, and all. I'm quite a whittler."

"I should say you are." Mrs. Parker glanced at her wrist watch, which showed that the time was slipping away too fast, and stood up preparing to leave. "It's a beautiful boat model and we've enjoyed having you tell us about it."

The old man nodded his head slowly. "Beautiful and useful," he said solemnly, "like any good boat."

Walking back to the car after saying good-by, Tony wondered what Mr. Bingham meant by saying the *Edna M.* model was useful as well as beautiful. Maybe it was just an odd fancy the old man had. It was nice to have for a decoration, but he couldn't see anything useful about it.

Later, as the car swung off the river-bottom road onto the highway, Mrs. Parker leaned back with closed eyes. "We've had a full day," she said in a tired voice. "Too bad we didn't accomplish our purpose in coming out here."

"Bentley said it was a wild-goose chase," Tony sighed.

"Oh, that Bentley!" Lynn exploded. "What does he know about it?"

Without taking her eyes from the road, Mrs. Wilson chided her daughter gently. "Come down off your high horse, honey. For my part, I've had a wonderful time. If you folks should ever decide to go back for another search, just let me know."

Everyone lapsed into silence. Even Co-Co seemed weary and worn out with the excitement of the day. They were almost home, and it would be good to get back.

Driving along the tree-lined street, suddenly above the sound of the motor there came the deep tones of a bell ringing steadily. No one in the car could quite believe his ears. It sounded like the bell on top of the carriage house.

CHAPTER

13

THE PEAL OF THE
bell continued with steady persistency.

" Is that the signal bell? " Cherry gasped.

" There's one way to find out," Tony muttered between clenched teeth. " Let's go! "

Mrs. Wilson turned the corner and pressed down on
the gas. Even with increased speed, Tony felt as if the
car were creeping. " Hurry, hurry, hurry," he murmured under his breath.

" Now just calm down." His mother drew him firmly
back beside her. " We're not going to break the speed
limit, or break our necks either."

The next moment they caught sight of the Parkers'
car coming toward them from the corner and entering
the winding driveway that led to the house on the hill.
They turned in right behind it.

" Guess Dad was home from the office." Cherry
clutched Co-Co excitedly.

" Wherever he was," Tony said hoarsely, " he didn't

lose any time getting here."

When Mrs. Wilson turned off the motor at the top of the hill, Mr. Parker slammed his car door shut and came rushing toward them with a puzzled look on his face. " So it wasn't any of you ringing the bell. I thought maybe you had stopped back here on your return from the river."

He wheeled abruptly at the sound of a dog's excited barking. " That sounds like Skipper! " he bellowed, and strode swiftly around the house.

The others poured out of the car and hurried after him, completely forgetting that they were tired.

" Bentley! " they heard him shout in amazement. " And Skipper! What in the world are you doing here? "

His face paler than usual, Bentley dashed forward, stumbling as he ran. " I thought somebody ought to be watching the place," he panted. " That's why I didn't go to the river. Skipper and I have been walking up and down the street — " he paused for breath. " It's a good thing too. From the corner at the top of the hill, I saw a man running from the carriage house to the back door. He's in the house now. So I rang the bell."

Just then he saw his mother and father coming across the garden, looking frightened and anxious. He hoped they would understand why he had come to the hill. Skipper had been with him all the time; there was no danger with Skipper around. Even if he had called him a mutt, he was a truehearted, courageous, loyal mutt.

" Bentley! " his mother cried out frantically. " Are you all right? "

Bentley had no time to answer, for at that moment

142

they all turned to stare as a young man walked down the back steps and came toward them — a young man in uniform, with waving blond hair and a wry smile on his face.

" George! " Cherry shrieked, running to meet him with Co-Co clinging to her shoulder.

" Hello, Cherry darling." At the sound of his voice, the monkey leaped from her shoulder into the young man's arms. He scratched the fuzzy head affectionately. " How're you, Pee-Wee? Ran away from me, didn't you? But I see you've been in good hands."

Cherry's eyes widened. " Is Co-Co your monkey? "

George Fellows nodded. " He was mascot on our ship, and they gave him to me when we docked at San Francisco." He looked from one to another of the astonished group. " I'm sorry to have caused so much disturbance. I suppose I've been pretty stupid, but it seemed the only thing to do at the time."

Mr. Parker stepped forward. " We're all mighty glad to see you." He extended his hand in greeting and smiled ruefully. " So you're the mysterious intruder! "

" You? " Tony began, then stopped openmouthed at the wailing sound of the police car siren coming nearer.

Mr. Parker excused himself and hurried out front to meet Sergeant Thomas and Officer Edwards as the siren came to a whining halt. The men talked together for several minutes, while Mr. Parker explained the latest developments, before they joined the group.

" Well," Sergeant Thomas observed, dabbing at his forehead with a big white handkerchief, " pleased to meet you, George. I'm glad there was no foul play connected with this."

143

"Thank you, sir," George replied with an embarrassed smile. "I'll try to explain everything."

"When did you get home?" Mr. Parker asked gently, trying to put him at ease.

"I've been here since the night Bentley saw the flashlight in Dad's study," George said, his smile beginning to relax into its natural good-humored curve. "I overheard you talking about whether or not it was his im-

144

agination while I hid in uncomfortable silence."

"Then Bentley was right!" Tony's voice rang out triumphantly as his friend flushed at these welcome words of vindication.

"So right," George agreed.

"Bentley never misses a trick," Mr. Adams said, beaming at his son with warm approval.

"I had fifteen days leave before being transferred," George went on, "and I wanted to get some of my personal belongings here in the house. I understood that I wouldn't be allowed to enter until the estate was settled, so I thought the simplest thing to do — foolishly, perhaps — was to go in through the basement window that had a broken lock."

"Then it was you who left that window open?" Officer Edwards smiled.

George nodded. "You see, I had a set of keys, but I left them with Dad for safekeeping and he told me he would keep them in his study desk. That's what I was looking for the night these folks came up to investigate. There was a key to the carriage house, so Pee-Wee and I would dash out there when anyone came up the hill." He grinned and rubbed his hand over Tony's tousled head. "Provided we had time. These loyal caretakers almost caught up with me, and I couldn't scare them away even by leering at them through the keyhole of the carriage house door."

Tony was beginning to see the pieces of the puzzle fall into place. The picture was growing clearer when another thought struck him. "Then those were your fingerprints on the piano!" he burst out.

"I'm afraid so," George admitted. "I opened it and

145

played late at night when I thought no one was likely to be around."

"Well," Sergeant Thomas said, mopping his forehead again, "everything seems to be cleared up except the whereabouts of the will. Is that right?"

Tony's shoulders drooped wearily. "The red-haired man, Mr. Hardesty, said it was in the *Edna M.* — but it wasn't."

"I didn't think it would be," Bentley said in a clear, firm voice. "I always thought the model of the *Edna M.* on Captain Gabe's desk was the perfect place to hide a will."

Lynn stared at the competent look on his face. A new feeling of respect for Bentley was beginning to dawn in her mind. While he seemed to be critical and un-co-operative, he was really thinking sharper than any of them — just like a real detective. Maybe he was right about the will.

"But we peeped in and there was nothing there." Tony's voice was dismal. "Don't you remember? It was just hollow."

George handed the monkey to Cherry, a faraway look on his face. "As I recall," he began, his brow creased in thought, "that model had a false bottom." He snapped his fingers. "Yes, it did! Could we go up and see?"

"Certainly," Mr. Parker answered quickly, since the question was directed at him. "I have permission from the court to search for the will. Let's take a look right now."

Mrs. Adams, who had been talking quietly with the other two women, stopped the eager departure for a minute. "Hold on, please," she said brightly. "I know you're all tired and hungry. Mrs. Wilson and Mrs. Parker have said they'll go home with me and we'll fix something to eat. I cooked a big roast and made a cake today, so there's enough for everybody."

Her invitation was accepted with enthusiasm by all except the officers, who said they'd had their supper and must stay on duty.

Mrs. Adams hesitated a moment and looked directly at George. " We'd like to have you come to our house and be our guest for the rest of your visit. There's an extra bedroom and I think you'll be more comfortable than you have been, staying here without any conveniences."

When George caught the look of breathless expectancy on Bentley's thin face, he answered appreciatively: " That's very kind of you, Mrs. Adams. I'll be glad to stay with you if you don't mind having another man underfoot for a day or so."

" That'll be swell." Bentley breathed happily.

Mrs. Wilson's car drove away, and the searching party entered the back door, with George leading the way to Captain Gabe's study on the second floor.

" Do you suppose," Cherry whispered to Tony, " that Captain Gabe really meant the boat model when he told Mr. Hardesty the will was safe in the *Edna M.?* "

" Come to think of it," Tony replied, " I really do. If he'd meant the big boat, he'd have said *on* the *Edna M.* — not *in.*"

Inside the study, everyone watched with increasing excitement as George reached for the boat model on top of the desk. His face was tense. " Would two of you please help me turn it over? "

With the aid of Mr. Parker and Sergeant Thomas, the boat model was turned upside down and the two men held it firmly. George moved his hand over the wooden bottom and it slid beneath his touch, revealing an inner compartment holding a folded blue paper.

George drew it out and read aloud. " Last Will and Testament of Gabriel S. Fellows." The paper crackled in the waiting silence as he unfolded it, then glanced at Mr. Parker, who was replacing the heavy model with the assistance of Sergeant Thomas. " I guess it's all right for me to look at this? " There was a noticeable huskiness in his voice.

Mr. Parker nodded. " I think it would be proper for you to read it, since you have witnesses. Then it must go to the court to be probated."

George read in an undertone. " I hereby revoke all former wills made by me." He bit his lower lip and finished reading the rest of the first page silently. After a few seconds, he lifted his eyes from the paper. " Dad left the *Edna M.,* this house, and its furnishings to me. Everything else to be divided equally among his three children."

" Then you'll come back here to live someday? " Cherry burst out, unable to control her delight at the prospect.

George seemed lost in thought and did not answer her immediately. He folded the paper without reading farther and handed it to Mr. Parker. " Will you see that this is properly taken care of, sir? " Then turning to Cherry, he said softly, " Yes, honey, as soon as my enlistment is over, I'd like to come back here to live — forever."

" Well, now that everything is settled," Tony said, heaving a deep sigh, " let's go get something to eat."

As they left the house after locking up, Officer Edwards fell in step between Tony and Cherry. " How's Co-Co? " he asked, patting the monkey's head as he rode on Cherry's shoulder. " Is he behaving himself? "

" Oh, sure." Cherry smiled up at him. " Only his name is really Pee-Wee and he belongs to George."

" So we won't have him much longer," Tony added. " We wanted to have him in our pet show."

George overheard the conversation and turned around. " Co-Co is a better name for him. Let him keep it — he doesn't seem to mind the change. In fact, he seems so contented, I may leave him here with you if your mother will agree to it."

" Then he can be a member of the Be Dramatic Club," Tony beamed. " We'll tell you more about that later." He glanced at Lynn, who was thinking the same thing he was — thinking about shows in the carriage house!

CHAPTER

14

WHEN THEY LEFT
the hill, everyone went home first to clean up for the
dinner at Bentley's. It was going to be a gala occasion.
Even Co-Co and Skipper were included with the guests,
for Mrs. Adams hailed Tony and Cherry as they left
Bentley at his back door and were hurrying with their
father toward the gate in the hedge.

"Bring Skippy and Co-Co when you come back," she
called out, her cheeks pink with excitement. "They've
been part of the adventure and should have a share in
the celebration."

Tony smiled up at his dad after stammering his
thanks. "She's not a bad sort, is she?" he whispered,
hurrying on.

His dad's answering smile was full of understanding.

Finally the crowd gathered together in the Adams
cool, spacious dining room. The boys looked dapper
and neat with slicked-down hair and fresh summer
slacks. The girls had agreed previously to dress alike as

nearly as possible, so Lynn wore a red pleated skirt and her new white sweater with the red and black poodles embroidered on the front. Cherry's crisp white blouse and red plaid skirt made the girls feel like twins. Bentley eyed Lynn's sweater for a brief instant, then made a special point of expressing admiration as he pulled out a chair for her to be seated.

Skipper was on his best behavior and lay quietly at Tony's feet, while Co-Co perched on the back of George's chair.

Jovial and smiling, Mr. Adams carved the roast, and during the meal there was much joking and laughter as the adventures of the past few days were recalled and lived over.

When the dish of green onions, fresh from the Parkers' garden, was passed around, Cherry said with sly humor: " Don't give George any onions. He doesn't like 'em. He ate his hamburger but he left the onions on his plate in the basement."

" This beats eating hamburgers." George smiled, looking from one friendly face to another. " And it beats eating alone in the basement."

When Mrs. Adams served her cake, piled high with golden sliced peaches and mounds of whipped cream, Co-Co, who had been very well behaved during the main course of the meal, reached down and pulled a handkerchief out of George's coat pocket. Everyone burst out laughing when he solemnly wiped his funny little face.

" He's imitating Sergeant Thomas," Cherry cried out gaily. " If he keeps on learning tricks, he'll be the best actor in the pet show."

After the laughter subsided, Tony looked at his mother questioningly. " George says we may keep Co-Co if it's all right with you."

Mrs. Parker clasped her hand to her brow in mock alarm. " Good gracious! " she smiled wryly. " Don't we have enough pets with Skipper and Eloise? "

" But he's so cute," Cherry sighed as George took back his handkerchief. " Anybody would like to have him."

" I'd like to have him," Bentley sputtered, his fork clattering to the plate. He lifted pleading eyes to his mother's face. " We just have one pet."

" That's right," Mrs. Adams agreed with unexpected enthusiasm. " And Calico Cat really belongs to me. If everyone is willing, Co-Co could be Bentley's own special pet."

" Hurray! " Lynn shouted. " It looks like — "

" Lynn! " Her mother interrupted, afraid that her daughter was about to needle Bentley in return for saying the monkey looked like her. " Where are your manners? "

Lynn sat up primly, her eyes twinkling. " I was just going to say it looks like Bentley will have the star performer in the show."

" I'll help you build a cage for him," Tony offered eagerly. " Officer Edwards told us exactly how to make one."

Mr. Adams reached over and clapped a plump hand on Bentley's shoulder. " There's plenty of scrap material where the carpenters have been working in the game room," he beamed. " If you don't find everything you need, I'll see that you get it."

Bentley swallowed hard to choke back the lump in his throat. Everything was turning out swell — simply swell.

The delicious meal was ended. At the suggestion of their parents, the children went outside with George to the front lawn, where fireflies were just beginning to flicker on and off in the fading twilight. Under the spreading oak tree, Cherry flopped to the ground with Skipper curled peacefully at her side. Tony and Bentley sat down opposite her on the grass, leaving the swing for Lynn and George. Co-Co nestled contentedly on Bentley's shoulder.

Through the deepening shadows, Tony gazed across the street at the majestic white columns of the house on the hill. " I'm glad Captain Gabe's house belongs to you, George," he said with a little catch in his throat. " When are you coming back here to live? "

" It won't be very long." George leaned forward in the swing, his earnest face soft with memories and dreams of the future. " When that time comes I hope to bring somebody with me. You see, my reason for being in such a hurry to get to New York is to see the girl I plan to marry. As soon as my enlistment is over, it would be wonderful to come back here to make our home."

Cherry cocked her head to one side and asked seriously, " Is she as nice as you are? "

" Much nicer," George assured her with a glowing smile. " You'll love Allene and I'm sure she'll love every one of you. I expect she'll want to join your club: she's enthusiastic about dramatics. That's her main interest."

" Good! " Lynn clapped her hands softly. " A new

153

member for the Be Dramatic Club. We used to meet in Bentley's basement until — " She stopped short at a queer choked sound from Bentley. " But we'll find another place before she gets here."

" Of course you will," George said heartily. " Maybe someday with Allene's help we could remodel the *Edna M.* and have a real showboat on the river. Until then, why not the old carriage house? I'd like you to use it."

There was a stunned silence. " What's the matter? " George lifted his eyebrows. " Don't you like my idea? "

Cherry began to giggle. " It's not your idea, George. It's ours! "

" We've been wanting to show Lynn the inside of the carriage house," Tony explained. " That's why we went to the hill that first night. She thought it would be a perfect place for a little theater."

George jumped out of the swing and took Lynn's hand, then lifted Cherry to her feet. " We'll show her right now." He turned at the sound of the screen door opening on the porch. " Here come your folks. Ask their permission and I'll run in and get my key and a flashlight."

He was back in a few minutes and off they went full of eager anticipation.

Mrs. Wilson and the Parkers sat down on the comfortable front porch with Bentley's parents, and smiled as they watched George and the four children with Skipper and Co-Co follow the wide, curving driveway to the house on the hill.

Biography of Vardine Russell Moore

The everyday fun — the hopes and heartaches, joys and disappointments — of being the oldest member of a large family started Vardine Russell Moore on her lifework with children and young people. The young Russells were brought up in sight of the Ohio River, first in Kentucky, then in Indiana, still Mrs. Moore's home today. After college she became a kindergarten teacher, at the same time writing and broadcasting a children's story hour. Later she worked as a scout leader, Sunday school teacher, and director of a private nursery school, writing children's stories constantly for *Jack and Jill, Child Life,* Sunday school and other publications. She is the author, in collaboration with Fleur Conkling, of *Billy Between* and *House Next Door,* and is married to an inventor who, she says, also likes to invent stories. The Moores have a teen-age daughter.